Volume Four

# THE CITY

Futura

AN ORBIT BOOK

This edition published in 1985 by
Futura Publications, a Division of
Macdonald & Co (Publishers) Ltd
London & Sydney

ISBN 0 7088 8140 8

Printed and bound in Great Britain by
Hunt Barnard Printing Ltd, Aylesbury, Bucks.

Futura Publications
A Division of
Macdonald & Co (Publishers) Ltd
Maxwell House
74 Worship Street, London EC2A 2EN

A BPCC plc Company

# PART ONE
# THE COLD LITTLE BROTHEL

A BIG sailor carried me on to the quay. He plonked me down. My knees folded.

I found I was sitting on a barrel, with sharp iron bands circling it. The sailor looked so huge, I must be feverish.

The quay-noises hit and broke on my head. The dirtiest quay I've ever been on. And a scum of dirty ice over almost everything, so even all the massive rope looked like ermine.

That boy from the ship appeared beside me. He set down a bucket of water. He broke the ice on it, and dipped in a bundled rag. He started to scrub my face with it.

I jumped up. I kicked the bucket over. My face burnt.

The boy looked reproachfully at me (I could see his yellow eyes through the briar-tangle of greasy curls).

'Cap'n ordered me to wash your face,' he told me.

'Where's my baby?' I demanded in the sudden panic with which I seem always to be demanding this.

'It's somewhere.'

'I want her. Have her brought.'

The captain shouldered between a man leading a thin nervous bull and a pedlar with a tray of trash.

'Is her face washed?' he asked the boy.

'I appreciate your concern for my personal hygiene,' I said, 'but if you give me my daughter, I'll find a lodging and you need trouble no further.

The captain peered closely at me. He ran a hand through my hair and let its texture slide across his attentive fingers. For all the notice he took of the words coming out of my mouth, they might have been inaudible as well as invisible.

'Get her on the stand,' he grunted at the boy. He shouldered away again through the crowd.

'He's got some treacherous plan, hasn't he?' I said to the boy.

'He's going to auction you here on the quay. He reckons he should get some payment for carrying you as passenger these past months.'

'But the bandit chief gave him money to pay my way – and my baby's. He was forbidden to harm me.'

'Oh, he's too afraid of that bandit bear to hurt you at all. He's simply finding you a good home, a haven like the bandit put it, and making a bit on the side.'

'I'll find my own haven.'

The boy got me to my feet. 'Pull your cloak closer,' he urged. 'You'll freeze.'

'And fetch a poorer price,' I finished.

The walk over the filthy cobbles was painful. 'I'm weak,' I said. 'Does he realise I've got scurvy? My food must have cost him nil.'

'It was bad for all of us,' the boy said.

Yes, only last night the ship had still tossed so I thought the last I should ever see of the world would be sea-storm.

'The storm lasted near a week,' the boy said.

'There were coils in the storm and spume, weren't there?' I said. 'We saw them from the port-hole . . . '

'Yes, serpents troubled from the deeps by the lightning,' he said.

The wharf-crowd reached a score of greasy hands to touch me but the captain and auctioneer bundled me up on the rostrum.

The captain scowled at me even before I gathered my strength to pant out, 'Ael will have your head piked for this.'

'I'm seeing you settled safe, aren't I? Stow it.'

'Sell my daughter with me.'

'Who wants your idiot child? Shark's meat, that's all.'

'Have you thrown her overboard?'

The captain shrugged, bored by a conversation so little connected with business. He wandered over to watch the auctioning already sponsored on the front of the rostrum.

'Please, please tell me – ' I clutched the boy's sleeve and

steeled my fingers not to let go when he twisted it. The cobbled darning parted, stitches dangling like mouldered lace. Again his small yellow eyes stared reproachfully out from the grease-tangle.

'Shall I see if I can find it?' he asked thoughtfully.

'You lovely boy. Please find her quickly and smuggle her to me – I'll hide her under my cloak and no one'll know – '

'The cap'n won't let a idiot baby spoil your value.'

'I've no value, I look like a famine-corpse,' I said. 'And because she can't speak, doesn't mean she's feeble in the head – '

'Hang on.' He loped off, eeling among the crowd. They call him Eel.

Pray my little God they've been too busy to chuck her over already.

Dimly I heard the bidding out front.

'Luverly yard-slave, muscles like metal . . . Fifty pieces . . . Who'll raise me ten pieces? Feel these muscles, any gent welcome to step up and judge for hisself . . . Going – Gone . . . Fine yearling colt, muscles like metal.' Clock of reluctant hooves on the hollow plank-platform, indignant whinny. They're auctioning horses and humans.

Before it was my turn, Eel had appeared beside me. He held something hidden in his voluminous patchwork poncho.

I stopped praying and dared not breathe.

'Is she alive?'

'You decide,' he said. He opened a slit in the poncho and let me see the pale still mite.

'Let me hold her – ' I ached open my arms.

'No.' A sly gleam enlivened the flat yellow eyes. 'I'll only give her to you if you let me help you escape.'

'What's the catch in this, Eel?'

'Hold on, hold your hurry. I just reckoned as you might like to escape. Any money on you?'

'The bandit gave me thirty pieces. Twenty are yours if you can fix me a get-away.'

'Hang on,' he promised.

'Is she alive, *tell* me?'

7

He poked her. She stirred.

The captain came up, pushed me forward. 'You're on.'

The captain pulled my hood back. The small needling winds shrilled my hair. I could feel the flame of my suddenly exposed ears.

'Young lady from Atlan 'erself,' intoned the auctioneer.

'Are they all that pasty-faced over there?' inquired one of the swaying audience.

'Breasts like cucumbers,' boasted the auctioneer. Under my thin cloak, they felt cooler. 'Honey hair.' They could see for themselves the fallibility of this claim, but they were all fascinated now that the auctioneer had got going. Possibly no one expected his lyrical rhetoric to have anything to do with grey reality. 'Navel holds an entire ounce of scent,' he ended.

There was a pause. With a faint stirring of hope, I thought no one would make an offer and the captain's goods would be left on his hands.

I couldn't, in this wind, believe how the wine-crates being un-trundled from the hold had been shipped simply for the heat of the passage, to braise in their barrels and return flavour-improved to their starting place. Anyway, perhaps as ballast they'd saved our lives in the storm-weeks, I thought – gratefully?

Then a voice said, 'Twenty pieces.'

I looked automatically for the owner of the voice, but couldn't fit a face to it, and someone else bid, and then they all started. The only other female on the rostrum, besides a dappled sow which did go for a sow-fat price, had been a bent sack-shape slave: more a beast of burden than a woman, all hopes and fears long since beat out of her. Women must be rare this season. In a proper slave-market I'd've been thrown in as a free extra with some other lot.

I looked about at the dirty quay. Three figures in long gowns with hoods had joined the back of the crowd. I couldn't tell if they were men or women, they seemed rather pot-bellied and not particularly dignified, but when the crowd noticed them too and became shifty and shuffled

8

and stopped spitting, I supposed the hooded figures must be priests.

Well, one thing I could tell.

Here, priesthood must be pretty sure of itself. For such big-bellied, greasy-gowned, slouching figures, these were starting big ripples of nervous respect across the quay. The hoods lifted and twitched, as if searching. Finally one priest raised a loose arm. From his sleeve, a pudgy gloved hand unfolded. It pointed. It pointed at a thug in a scarlet sash who went a nasty putty-colour and from whom the crowd drew away as if he had developed instant leprosy.

No soldiers were needed to enforce the priests' invitation. This I noted with an uncanny feeling at my spine. I've been in other cities where other priests have had their big say, but none other where the priests could pick out a man they wanted, who would turn odd with fear and go to them without being hauled by Temple soldiery.

The man and the priests diminished across the filthy ice.

The crowd seemed to expand as every chest heaved a sigh, all relief. A note of naturalness came back to the bidders' voices.

I was slumping, weary, weak, icy cold, but still the bidding continued. I sank to a seat on the top step of the rostrum. Nobody kicked me to stand up again, so I pulled my hood over my ears and listened to my faint thoughts (and absolutely empty stomach) till the bidding suddenly ceased.

The auctioneer's hammer vibrated. I dug in my head for an echo of the last bid. 'Ninety pieces,' some extravagant shopper had said.

A dark man in his thirties was making his way to the front of the crowd to claim me.

A greenish monkey kept its balance, clutching its mobile feet over his shoulder, tearing a fruit to bits in its hands, lifting its little sunken eyes ecstatically to the raw heavens, chattering its bright enamel incisors on fruit rind and pulp and spit and twitters of joy.

Just under the monkey's small happy mindless head, the man's dark thick hair fell like a bar across a strong sullen

9

face and two dark eyes glowing but without emotion of any kind.

*

My new owner's cart lurched and clattered down and up the stony alleys. Two piebald mules pulled it. The man slouched at the reins, his back and the monkey's back towards me.

The boy had been too late. He hadn't appeared in time to slip Seka into my arms, under my tattered cloak, before I was lifted into the back of the cart among hessian sacks. The dark man swung on to the drive-perch, the monkey chirruped like a bird, and the waterfront receded with its bleak sea-winds (small and multitudinous as the waves) and its execrable stinks. And here instead were the smells of slum alleys.

'Why did you buy me?' I asked the back.

'Why do you think?' he answered briefly.

This could mean anything. I could be put to any use he thought too matter-of-fact for mention.

Suddenly he swore into my next sentence and cut my question still-born.

We'd reached a cross-roads, cross-alleys rather. Rushing out from each of the four black apertures came a boy on foot. The boys were all brandishing cudgels and yelling extremely impractical threats. My master yelled too. The mules charged: that's the only word.

'Keep your head down,' he jerked at me. 'It's you they're after. We'll get by easily as long as they can't grab you. Lie flat – '

We were already half past them – but the two now behind were pursuing, the two in front determinedly blocking the path ahead.

'You mangy apes,' my master tossed at them (while the little one on his shoulder chattered its private delirium). 'Out of my way before I crush your flat heads on the bricks.'

This seemed a routine insult. But it enraged my abductors. Two of them hurled their heavy cudgels. Of

10

course they missed as we hurtled forwards at five miles an hour (unwieldy cart, mules deliberate even in rage).

'Now,' my master said calmly through the mule-squeals and cart-clatter, 'they've lost their bashers. Lie flat and we're through.'

And indeed the boys in front no longer blocked our way, They had to get out from our onslaught.

I lay flat and looked behind. And right into a pair of yellow glinting eyes.

At the last possible minute for such a risk, just as the mules decided to work up a savage gallop and the cart lurched as on high seas, I threw myself out of the cart. Or rather, I tumbled over the side and rolled on the cobbles.

Eel pounced on me. He dragged me into a doorway deep, dark and smelly as a cave.

The cart disappeared trundling terribly down an alley hill-steep. The man who'd bought me hadn't noticed my defection.

The pedestrians, who'd been patiently waiting to get by, now quietly got by.

'I thought you'd never latch on,' Eel panted. 'I thought you'd changed your mind and wanted to stay with him.'

'A thousand times thank you, Eel. Who are these other people? Did it cost you much to hire them?'

'They're me mates. This is me home-town, see.'

'How lucky I was to fall in with you, Eel. If you give me my baby, I'll give you my money.'

'The babby's at me Mam's house. Come to think,' he suddenly said, 'it just struck me like, you can't go wandering round in a strange city looking for lodging. You might get into all sorts of trouble. Why don't you stay at me Mam's?'

'Oh, Eel. Would she mind?'

'Pleased, delighted she'd be. You never met a lady more hospitable nor Mam.'

'It sounds too good to be true. Of course I'd pay her rent –'

'My Mam would throw it back if you offered it.

Offended, like. You know. Mam'll see you safe. Likely find you a nice job and all.'

The three other boys slouched up. Their first beards fluffed their chins – except for the youngest, whose voice was just beginning to break.

'This is Sausage, this be Garl, this here's me young brother Lud.' Eel made ceremonious introductions.

'Thank you so much, all of you,' I said earnestly. They'd retrieved their cudgels, but even with those they looked very young – and gallant to have tried stopping a man like my owner driving a big cart drawn by a brace of horrible mules.

They muttered unsmilingly that it had been nothing, but by their grunts and slight stammers I could feel their pride in themselves and their appreciation of my appreciation.

The alleys were a labyrinth. We wandered slowly and at ease through them. As the boys seemed in command of the situation, I didn't nervously remind them that perhaps my dark master, having learnt of his loss, would come after us and we should hurry to the haven of Eel's Mam's.

I felt terribly impatient to get to Seka.

I could imagine her dumb despair as once again she believed herself lost or abandoned by her mother. I longed almost hysterically to gather her up and croon and comfort her and make her feel that for a while again safety had happened.

It was an effort to keep quiet, not to nag my lovely noble rescuers to race and pelt to Mam's – not that I could have kept up anyway. I felt even weaker after the excitement. My heart kept hitting my ribs. My head spun, lights flashed across my eyeballs. But I felt light-headed and happy and without a care in the whole of the world, the whole of the beaming grimy brick darling universe.

'Isn't it nice, dry land instead of a storm-tossed ship?' I remarked to Eel.

'Here, you haven't eaten since your biscuits on board yesterday, have you?' he suddenly said.

'And they were weevilly.'

Lud, the young brother, grabbed a fruit off a pedlar's tray. The pedlar yelled and shook his big fist and started to chase, but fruit like big gaudy jewels began to roll and bounce off his neck-slung tray, and he gave up, cursing hoarsely. The boys gathered up the bruised fruit. They wiped off the gutter-slime and began gnawing through their cackles. Eel peeled a citrus for me.

The slums were getting worse. Ragged gaps gaped in the walls. Bricks were hardly more than rusty powder. The buildings leaned like drunken hags losing a grim battle to remain upright, retain dignity. The upper storeys jutted either side and nearly met. Splinters of grey winter sky were only just visible between them. The smells were stale as if we were indoors – in fact many alleys were more corridors than anything else, roofed by ancient stone, or by wooden arches with dropping-green rafters in which storks untidily nested, flapping, gossiping over our heads.

The pedestrians splashing with us through the open central street-drains were tattered, noisy, pungent, and inclined if they were men to slip an arm round any girl as she passed, or touch her here or there (mostly there). These were attentions my escort took for granted, and made no move to rebuff on my behalf. Sometimes a rider passed on a snorting slaver-toothy yellow-nostrilled red-eyed mule, scattering the walkers. There were a terrible number of cripples.

The wind was filmy. Really shreds of blown fog. Very clammy in my skirts. When something bowled against my shins I thought it another pedlar's gourd tossed by wind. Then I saw the unsighted eyes staring up at me, the rotted nostrils.

'A head – ?'

I was too surprised to be sick. This was surrealism.

'Blown off a pike,' said Eel. He pointed to the pikes with the warning heads of executed malefactors. 'Blasphemer's head.'

Presently the city humped. It shook itself into a convulsion of hills and valleys, razor-sharp bends, alleys twisting

13

and winding like spiral staircases, steps cut and now crumble-edged, pavements that were staircases of shallow platforms or steps so high they strained your groin to climb.

And finally alleys that were straight slopes, terribly steep, and you looked down and found you were panting over little dim barred windows staring up under your skirts, and these alley-pavements sloping underfoot were also the walls of dwellings.

And now we were by the Canal.

Steamy, sleazy garbage-green rotting water, if water can rot, splitting the houses off from each other.

'Mam's house overlooks the Canal,' Eel said.

'Oh?' I said politely.

From his simple pride, I gathered the Canal must be a sort of suburban area, a desirable residential area.

The width of the green water did space the buildings on the banks, so they no longer touched upper storey to upper storey rubbing beams, and there was room for balconies – even if the balconies were falling to one side so anybody standing on one would slide to the bottom end. The walls were plastered too, though the plaster was all diseased and scabrous, and slimy with fungus at the water-level.

The boys jumped into one of the boats jostling the tow-path. They handed me across the inches of Canal, bank to boat.

'A brass-coin each, ferry-fare,' the man said as he poled out into the trafficking, through the swashing rippling garbage.

'Yah, our patronage is enough advertisement to keep you happy,' the boys said and simply didn't pay.

Green ice still scummed parts of the back-waters I glimpsed here and there, but in the main the river was so alive it actually gave more an impression of warmth than the labyrinth we'd come through. The busyness seemed to engender its own humus.

I leant back on the slatted seat. I was exhausted. The boat expertly avoided bumps and crashes, though there seemed no organised traffic-rules on the water. Eel put his

14

raggy arm round me. He drew my head on to his shoulder-knob.

'Nearly home,' he promised.

\*

I was amazed by the grandeur of Mam's.

Velvet drapes, all the gear. Curtains shutting out the day-light and the ghastly view. A diffusion of candle-light.

The middle-sized room was full of layabouts, friends of Eel's and Mam's, men, women, girls – over a dozen people in their own fug, squirting pomegranate wine out of little bottles.

Hospitable, Mam, obviously.

Eel hurried me through this room, hardly greeting the languid paired-off 'company'. Extremely paired-off.

One woman, a heifer-woman, arose up slow and stately as a lily blossoming out of a lake, and followed us to the kitchen.

'I'm Rubila,' she said, her stiffened underclothes creaking lazily as her voice glided out from them.

'Me Mam,' Eel translated.

'It is terribly good of you to look after my baby – ' I began.

'You're staying here yourself, my Eel told me,' she raised her shaved brows.

'I thought you only just suddenly *thought* of asking your Mam to let me stay,' I remarked to Eel.

He shuffled his feet in the matting. But started on a defiant grin. He was on home-ground now.

'It is kind of your Mam,' I said to him while she stood gently creaking. 'But I'd sooner not trouble her. Perhaps she can recommend a regular Inn.'

'I'll get you work,' Mam said huskily.

'I don't do this kind of work,' I said.

I was searching round for a glimpse of Seka.

The kitchen was big and smoky – lit and warmed by braziers beam-slung – and full of tatty peeling screens which divided it into synthetic corridors and pantries and roomlets. Several slatterns slunk about, inhabitants here,

15

automatically yanking on the pump-handle, scraping vegetables, stirring cauldrons, poking fires, kicking kittens.

'Oh,' the big silky lady said, 'you won't be doing work of *this* nature. These are my menials. We wouldn't dream of working a person like yourself *this* way.'

She eyed me appraisingly. Her genteel accent, the sort that enunciates even the punctuation, said, *You and I are the quality class, you and I are.*

'I appreciate,' I remarked, 'that I wouldn't have been tricked into coming here, chasing after my baby and some extra promises, if you hadn't thought it would be a neat idea to get for nothing what the man with the monkey had to buy. I am not, however, going to work in your brothel.'

'Oh yes you are,' Mam said without a change of tone. 'You've no choice, darling.'

'Where's my baby?' I demanded loudly.

A girl undulated out of a corner, wiping Seka's tears on her savoury-stained apron.

I trembled with relief. At least the promise of Seka's being here wasn't a completely fake trick. At least my little voiceless burden, my poor little shadow, is still with me.

I snatched her from the gloom and the arms and the apron.

She stared. She flung her little hands against me, clutching my clothing, nearly banging my ribs. She hung on to me, all but digging herself into me, like a desperate parasite-plant.

'Give me some food,' I told the madam. 'I am weak. I think I have scurvy. I've had a terrible sea-voyage. You must give me something hot and filling or your customers will take one look and laugh.'

'I'll hot you some mutton,' she said. 'But mind. No ideas about making off now you've got your dumb dumpling. I'm putting you in a room with three other young ladies who'll see to it you don't stir a foot outside this place.'

She sailed beyond a screen or two.

'How did you suddenly discover we was a house of joy?' Eel demanded shiftily.

'The fondling and boozing, and even the décor, could

16

happen anywhere,' I admitted. 'But the sight of your Mam clinched it.'

'It's a fair old life for a young lady. You'll enjoy it once you're used to it. It's a home, isn't it? A bit of glamour. No hard graft. And little luxuries for you and Babby.'

'And disease and pot-bellied pathetics who can't get a girl unless they pay by the hour for one who is fastidious about nothing but wallet-sizes.'

'You'll be examined once a month,' Eel reassured me. 'It's easy cured in the early stages.'

Rubila slid alongside with a plate of gravy in which slopped mutton-slices, roast cheese-chunks.

'Has Seka been fed?' I asked after my first three or four incredible mouthfuls.

And they said Yes and hovered beaming at their new acquisition – skin and bone, but something for nothing, and soon to be fattened, and soon to be settled and resigned, and no chance of getting out even if not settled and resigned.

*

The first afternoon, after that mutton and that warning, they left me alone in the upstairs room with the four beds, one now mine (what happened to my predecessor?).

I settled Seka to sleep on my new off-white pillow, tucking the rugs and goatskin up around her. *She* is perfectly happy now, but won't let go my finger till deep asleep.

I found the Diary in my cloak-pocket. On board, in the sickness and storm, I lost my sticky-tipped scriber, but here I had found a quill-pen in the kitchen. I didn't quite dare beg Eel or Rubila for ink in case they thought I was preparing some sort of detailed documentary spy-indictment I hoped to work against them – but I did discover, delighted, a little leather sac of ink in one corner of a shelved chest up here. I have balanced the sac so it stays stiff and upright.

The familiar physical rhythm of writing is keeping my mind off this absolutely revolting situation.

There's no help for it just yet. Till some further development, or till I can explore a bit perhaps, there's no way I can get out.

*

I pretended to be asleep when the door opened, and I held the baby in one of those tight cuddles, willing her to feel so secure and mother-wrapped that she wouldn't wake even at the new noise and light.

Footsteps stumbled in. The straw-stuffed mattresses wheezed. There were all the predictable sounds, multiplied two maybe three times.

The door squealed again. Seka stirred. One person stumbled in, male or female, I couldn't tell because of the drunken heavy steps.

Whoever it was lurched on to a bed. Must have fallen on a busy couple. Giggling. Curses.

'Who'shat inna window bed?' a woman's voice slurred.

'New girl.'

'She'll soon end with pneumonia in that old sack. Tinia lasted a year in that bed.'

'No, it was the act with the donkey finished Tinia. The clients loved it. They only had to watch. That donkey's too big, even for Tinia. I tell you, whoever takes that donkey on is under death sentence.'

I lay very still. I tried to fake a sleeper's breathing.

'Kick the cow. Let's hear what she says for herself.'

'Oh, we'll have enough of her soon. Crawl away. Let workers sleep.'

'Oh, so thash wha' you call it, is i'?' The prostitute began another long crazy giggle.

Someone threw something heavy at her. A boot maybe. This set her off again. She rocked, screaming laughter. Seka's fingers twitched in on her sleeping palms. A man growled into someone's muffling hair, 'Can't someone strangle your friend?' 'That's right, darling, *you* take time off,' screamed the screamer. She lurched over and started prodding me.

'Wake up, new girl. Tell us your name, new girl.'

18

I couldn't pretend sleep as her fingers, point-nailed, stabbed in here and there.

'You wake my baby,' I said, turning to look at her though I couldn't make her out with the candle behind her, 'and I'll see Rubila makes your coming week hell.'

'Oh, we're Mummy's favourite, are we?' she said and she slumped away.

*

The dawn and I together slipped out of the sleeper-strewn dormitory. This time this door was unlocked. With Seka down the stairs.

I avoided the big ground 'company' room. And the door to the kitchen.

Another little door seemed ajar. I tiptoed over to it.

It slammed behind me. I was in another part of the kitchen. A thin boy, about eight, danced and cackled by the door he'd pushed.

'Trying to make your get-away?' he yelled.

I looked anxiously round. The kitchen-females made no sign as they mooped about their tasks, in and out between fogs of cooking-smoke and laundry-garlanded screens.

'Any breakfast, luv?' I asked.

'Let me have the young'un,' he said trying to grab her, peering into her face. Snot hung from his nostril and he breathed noisily on her through open-work teeth.

'No, you find us food,' I said.

'Foowoowoood – ' he yodelled, batting his hands before his mouth. One of the females cocked an eye at us under her greasy hair and started gathering up scraps of bacon.

'You like it here?' the boy asked. 'Do you like it here?' I intercepted the worms of bacon he was trying to stuff into Seka's mouth.

'No,' I said shortly.

'It's a good life,' the boy said in a confidential voice, peering now at me. 'A good time you'll have once you're used to it. This your first House?'

'You'd like it, I suppose,' I said.

'She tried to get me in on that side,' he agreed. 'Eel

19

wouldn't have it, and ran off to sea. So shall I when Summer comes. A dead loss it be on the waterfront. They don't tip me, the sailors, when I tell them, because they all know about this place already. And I'm not going in the business. It's painful for me, you see.'

'It's painful for me, too.'

'But you've had a kid and all,' he said, surprised. 'You a freak or such?'

'What's your name? Lud? I'll see you get a good place on a good boat,' I solemnly promised, 'if you ever see a way of getting me out of here.'

He put his head back and laughed.

A woman shuffled up with some milk which Seka seized on, her mouth opening as her hands reached.

I had to brush a hairy drowned fly off the milk before it gulped into Seka's mouth.

'Your cuisine will have us dead in a half-year,' I remarked.

'But you'll soon pick up a tapeworm off of Mam's pickled pork,' the boy said. He said it in an encouraging, congratulatory way.

'That will be jolly,' I agreed.

'Don't you know how healthful they be?' he bit off a hang-nail and spat it towards the porridge, but inefficiently missed. 'Worm looks after your health all right. Worm takes all the toxics out of your food and leaves the nutrition clear yours.'

The boy leaped on to the rim of a huge rust-crusted cauldron of stew swinging by a chain over an open hearth. He was like leather with springs in. His toes, heels, knees and elbows were tough as old rind. He balanced, cackling, his little yellow eyes still as flat as his brother Eel's little yellow eyes.

'Do yourself a favour,' he said to me, wasting time on me. 'Count your blessings. Little luxuries you'll be able to shower on the kid. We got a bath here, you know. Four-poster bath, with curtains. You can stay clean. The gentlemen know the girls here is clean, just like they know they won't never be rolled here even if they leaves their gold

20

parings, their silver slivers and their brass bitsies in their pockets while they buys their pleasure. No one can't catch nothing off of our girls. You're inspected every month. You can last ages.'

'I don't like men,' I said, bile rising in my throat. I had to talk slowly, careful. 'I'm sick if men touch me.'

'So we see,' he nodded at Seka.

'Her father too. And particularly the sort who have to come to places like this.'

'We'll see,' he grinned. 'Eh, Babby?'

*

As the woman plastered her patent beauty-air on my hair, my eyes travelled her big parlour.

Empty at noonday of company, the swathed drapes and tassels were tatty, stained with splashes of this and that which on some convivial evening had been splashes of booze or etcetera made in laughing abandoned jollity. The little stage was empty, dust rolled coagulated on the boards. Rubila might not mind endangering her wards' health with donkey-work, but at least that paid. No one wanted to pay to see goose bumps. The vaudeville season wasn't till Summer.

Between my knees was the pail of strong-smelling lardy stuff she kept dipping her spatula in to spread my hair with.

'What is it?' I asked.

'Dried mules' urine the stable-bloke sells me. Bleaching your hair. The gentlemen like the ladies blonde.'

'My hair's always been fairly fair,' I said.

'You're lucky having my guiding expertise. I'm at work on you now,' she said. 'You'll end a real doll, pretty as a puppet,' and she shaved my brows off and painted in swooping arches instead with a fine green brush.

When she'd piled my hair on my head, letting only one curl dangle artlessly, scraping rather rusty chiselled-tin fancy combs against my scalp to keep my hair neat, she pushed me to a fly-spotted mirror.

Beside her face, not my own. Now a tart's face. How easily I look a tart. Yellow hair and fine green brows and

21

suddenly the few times I've been to bed, I mean to bed with a man – and let's not forget I'm a legal wife – turn into a backlog of promiscuity in my face. I can't help returning a smile at the woman's triumphant reflection.

'Now don't you jiggle about,' she warned, 'not even tonight, not unless they pay you extra for it. A hairstyle like that takes some styling. Make it last a couple of weeks before it's to be done again.'

'Yes, you've done your best.'

'Now you wait for tonight. Wait till they come panting in. Wait till I introduce my new young lady. You wait, my girl.'

I'm her girl.

\*

Waiting, because there is nothing else to do, in the grand lewd draped best-barn. The other girls stitching last night's ripped décolletage. Laying stitches on stockings which must serve another fortnight at least. Repairing the pulled bobbles on a trouser-hem.

'They must be very rough . . . ' I say.

'They're paying for it,' a sallow woman answers sensibly.

It's all a transaction. Perhaps if I can just keep that in my head . . . After all, it's a reasonable transaction. The sense in it is old as hollow hills.

They want it. Why should they not buy what they want?

\*

But as the first customers began to arrive, I forgot my concentrated-for sanity.

The girls swooped on the first comers. A swarthy man because he is a good laugh, a sullen sour thin man with a stomach like an adam's apple on a thin throat, because he is a generous tipper to make up for his lack of small talk, his taciturnity which is really shyness. 'He's so shy he feels he must apologise for hisself even to the last-resort he's *paying* not to notice how gungy he is,' Lud sidles to my ear. 'See how such respectable citizens respect us? Ho no. You mustn't never feel you're at society's bottom. As a

22

whore, you be gone right up in the scale. You'd be surprised, luv,' said the pompous brat hooking thumbs in his belt, 'the respectabiggle wives who wish *they* was the hussy their old man sneaks off to every night.'

Nevertheless, I was gladder and gladder as each new arrival was nabbed by a quick girl – and then the first girl upstairs hurried, so energetic the nesting mice leaped frightened out of her stiffened hair, and was down again in a hustle of petticoats to look after a fresh customer just as I thought we'd run out of girls and it was finally my turn.

The girls turned See,-you're-not-doing-so-good looks on me.

I sat beside the sniggering boy and began to feel a bit safer – every extra five minutes of my cleanliness mattered before it was destroyed – and the girls went on making sure they pinched my privileges, working themselves sore taking on my sweated labour as well as theirs, making sure I was humiliated.

Finally one of the girls took pity on me. She came over in a flurry of powder and petticoats.

'You're supposed to get up and grab,' she told me kindly.

I looked at her and she smiled. She looked younger and less hard than the others. 'You're quite welcome to your suave glamorous customers, thanks luv,' I said and she flushed deeply under the crumbs of paint.

'Do you hate it?' she said ingenuously. 'I hate it. Do you wish you was out of it? Oh, what a life if you've been brought up nice like I was brought up nice. Oh, the shame of it. Oh, what would our Mams say if they could see us?'

I imagined what mine would perhaps say.

'Eel's Mam has her own ideas on the way to make youngsters useful,' I said.

'I can see you're brought up proper, just like me,' she said earnestly. 'My name's Aka. Can I be your friend? I'll take on the gentlemen you should take, till you feel you can bear it.'

'You poor child,' I said gently. 'How did you get into this?'

She liked me saying this, and I took care to sound even

23

more sincere than I felt. Now she was part of a conspiracy, the two girls who know they are a bit better than the other sluts. She gave me a terribly refined genteel smile to seal our pact, and hurried off to work.

But Rubila hadn't come through yet. She'd soon set things to rights.

I only prayed I'd be fairly lucky in the lottery.

A group entered. The girls converged on them like a flock of signpost arrows, straight to the mark, tireless. You had to admire their stamina.

Suddenly I thought, I'm mad.

I'm letting this group of boys be shared out. I can't go on being lucky. I'll get the next arrival – some wizened old paunch. And I'll've missed some likely lad, perhaps my only chance all night of a handsome boy. And with luck I could spin him out and make him last a whole night – I'm not interested in shoving as many tippers as possible into the time.

I got up and headed to the group.

Lud clapped his appreciation. 'You've got the idea at last, luv. Crowd the cows.'

The girls tightened at my approach. They began tossing heads and jingling earrings, making airy ladylike gestures, crooking little fingers.

'You'll have me,' I said to a tall wide-shouldered boy.

He grinned at me. He turned to grin at his mates. They slapped him on the back. He put an arm round me and we walked to the stairs – I'd forgotten the direction, but he knew it.

'Nerve. It's Shakina's go. That was Shakina's turn,' a woman with long bleached ringlets said.

Shakina tapped my boy's wide shoulder. She had long silver nails. 'You're my turn, dear,' she said.

'Oh, I'm spoken for,' the boy said. He tightened his amused flattered arm round me.

Upstairs, the long corridor seemed to shift, coiling like a serpent, the light of the only candle jerking the shadows.

'I think it's this door –'

'Yes,' he said. 'It is.'

He opened the door. We went into the room. My window-bed was empty. I led him to it between the other beds all grunting and creaking.

'You're new, I suppose,' he said.

At last I looked at his face. Downstairs, as I steeled myself to accost him, his face had been a blur. I'd picked out the nearest boy, that was all.

He had a handsome conceited face. More conceited now, I suppose. He thought I'd purposely picked him. He had thick sandy hair, too orangey even to be ginger. He wore a matching twin-set cloak and tunic, both pink-patterned with a trellis of stylised green vine-leaves, heavily fringed with tarnished tassels. The tassels were coming unravelled. He wore a big cloak-brooch studded with glass rubies, and a weapon-belt of stiff new leather with a dagger-sheath also studded with rose-tinted glass. He advanced on me and kissed me sloshily.

I returned the kiss all dutiful. Then I pulled away.

'What's your name?' he asked.

The kiss had told me he was less experienced than he took care to act. Probably he, like the elder men, came here only because he couldn't get the girls of his neighbourhood to co-operate. Now he'd thought, because I'd pulled away, a bit of polite chat was called for to show me he wasn't just some crude lout. He felt under the well-brought-up boy's obligation to waste time as well as money.

'Cija,' I said.

Perhaps he even had a Diary at home, and he noted names in a list he gloated over on rainy evenings.

'You're unusually nice, to find in a place like this,' the boy said.

'I am absolutely dead certain,' I said drily, 'that you say that to all the young ladies. And your little friends are saying that this minute to the ladies they've drawn out of the hat.'

'I'm not on my first visit here, you know,' the boy said with dignity. 'I've been here before,' he said with simple pride. 'On the whole, the girls here are a nice lot.'

'Good-hearted,' I agreed.

25

'That's it, hearts of gold,' he said eagerly. 'People think prostitutes are monsters.'

'But you've discovered they're people,' I interpreted.

'That's right, they're *people*,' he said warmly, as though he had once thought there was something else they might have been.

'Aren't you going to ask my name?' he said. 'If you like, when I come again I'll book for you.'

'You're rushing things,' I said coldly. 'You haven't found out what you think of my performance.'

'I'll take your shift off for you,' he offered.

'I'm not playing,' I said.

He looked at me, not getting it.

I sat on the bed. I said in a low voice, not that anyone else was bothering to listen anyway, 'Sorry. I thought I could do it. I can't after all.'

'You want to put the price up . . . ' he said uncertainly.

'No. But you were to have been my first patron. Congratulations. Except I can't do it. I thought I could. I can't bring myself to – '

'Why did you go in for this?' he asked intently, with all the middle-class boy's interest in social problems, where an older man would have forced his money's worth from me or clumped off in annoyance to wait a turn at the next bed.

'I didn't,' I said. 'I was sold into it. Yesterday.'

'Have you nowhere to go if you walk out?'

'That wouldn't stop me,' I said. 'If I *could* walk out. But they've got a sharp watch on to stop me. They lock doors on me. And I've a baby I can't leave.'

'You really want to get out? You're not a prostitute at all?' the boy said, becoming romantic under the orange hair, I could tell, about every boy's favourite romantic subject, the pure-souled slightly shop-soiled female in distress.

'Gods,' I said. 'Oh, yes, I want to get out.'

'Me and the boys'll work it,' he said.

Fate had her narrow spiteful eyes closed when she allowed me to go desperately to a callow boy I simply couldn't quite bring myself to lie back for, rather than to

26

some older man who would have managed the transaction for me.

*

But this Miyak managed things fine, anyway. A bit of unnecessary melodrama. Still, though I was afraid he'd mess the whole project and I'd have to stay here after all just because of his stage-managering, I was glad he enjoyed it.

'Wait there,' he said in a voice so much lower than he'd been using, I was sure the other beds would get suspicious, 'I'll go and round up the boys.'

'That'll be difficult – ' I said. 'They'll be in so many different beds. Do you need them all?'

He caught my hands in his. Directed an earnest gaze deep into mine.

'Just leave everything to me,' he said. 'I'll have you out. By the way, my name's Miyak.'

He gambolled off, as fast as if it were a matter of life-and-death, and happy as a hero. He knocked his shin against a bed-post but even that was in the line of front-line duty.

'Miyak!' I called.

Girls and patrons surfaced all around, to watch with interest in case I were going to bawl out my customer for short-changing me.

He came back obediently.

'I have a baby girl,' I said. 'She's being nursed in the kitchen by a girl with no front teeth.'

'You won't leave without her,' my hero promised in a conspiratorial tone. He shook hands with me, using some secret finger-sign I'm sure he didn't expect me to return. And I'm glad all the heads had submerged again as he laid his finger to his lips before bounding off again to my rescue.

I sat up on the bed. As the other girls one by one finished and scurried down to grab the next fee, they looked curiously at me. No one said anything. They thought I didn't realise I couldn't just sit waiting for my next man, but they certainly weren't going to tell me.

But while I waited, Rubila appeared.

A dark man was with her.

'So here you are,' said Rubila giving me a funny look. 'This is Gurul. Look after him to the best of your ability. He's my guest. I promised you to him on the house.'

She teetered over to whisper in my ear, 'Don't be nervous. He looks kinky but he's not too bad.'

The dark man bowed slightly.

'Gurul, Cija,' Rubila introduced all arch. She sailed away. 'No hard feelings,' back floated Rubila's syrup voice.

'At first I didn't recognise you without a monkey on your head.'

'You're pleasantly disguised yourself,' he said.

Pleasantly disguised eh? The man had no taste. I admit I looked a sad drab when he brought me. But now I looked so much trumpery.

After these conversational preliminaries, I simply looked nervously at him.

But he made no move.

'I'm glad I wandered in here tonight,' he said. 'One of Rubila's girls told me of a very new acquisition. I asked Rubila about it – and Rubila pretended there was no new girl. So of course then I knew who had relieved me of my goods yesterday. I threatened Rubila with the law – the ship's captain who sold you to me on that shit-freezer quay would have stood witness – and she turned hostess. No hard feelings, she says, all a little prank. But you're still legally mine. Legally.'

'You're a rival madam,' I said.

He didn't look insulted, yet I didn't think he looked queer either.

'I'll wager Rubila has you well stashed away by tomorrow, though,' he said. 'She knows I can't walk out with you tonight, since I dropped in unprepared, alone. And her ugly offspring and guards are at the doors. But she knows equally well that by tomorrow I'll be along with my own gentlemen.'

'You're going to come back to claim me, then?'

'I like your tone of surprise,' he said, rather sourly.

'What do you expect? You're entitled to be modest, but not stupid.'

'I just thought I'm – '

'Hardly worth the risk of broken heads? You're right. But I bought you cheap just because you looked such a scarecrow. And I'm not having my bargaining wasted. Anyway, you're a new face. A good few times, I'll be able to pass you off as a virgin, for double the normal price. We'll just keep sewing you up again. What's more, I'm not letting that painted old chimpanzee steal my property and crow about it afterwards.'

I thought I'd sooner belong to Rubila. This man, un-luckily my legal master, looked so nasty when he spoke of his stolen property, his jeopardised pride. His black eyes narrowed. Nasty lines appeared by his black nostrils.

I'm sure he was about to go. I know he wasn't the slightest bit interested in availing himself of Rubila's on-the-house offer. But just as he rose, just at this inauspicious moment instead of five minutes later, the gallant boy Miyak reappeared.

I was quite glad now that he'd spent so much trouble collecting all his mates. There were about eight of them, and by his own admission my master Gurul doesn't fancy violence when outnumbered.

Miyak stopped.

He went pink.

'Oh, you're busy – ' he said.

'I'm not,' I said quickly. 'I told you, I don't want customers.'

'Then who – '

'What is this?' Gurul said with that nasty look. 'Surely you don't take on a dozen at once?'

'She doesn't. Do *you* want to, mate?' asked a lovely boy with belligerent fists.

'You're planning escape tonight,' Gurul deduced. 'You've got hold of some lad with high principles from the suburbs and you've given him a sob-story. I know all you girls' little tricks. I'd better tell my hostess – '

'Oh, no, you don't,' said Miyak. The boys fell on Gurul

29

– to the amazement of the occupied beds. These were good boys, well-trained with their fists, but not experienced at dealing with real incidents not just practice-bouts. They didn't think to clamp his mouth, and Gurul raised a yell as they uselessly grabbed his wrists and legs.

The girls in the other beds also raised a yell, and a few patrons did up their trousers and buckled their belts and came over to interfere.

The girl Aka surfaced from one of the beds. One man gripped her: on her other side, her last customer lay still snoring, one heavy leg still sprawled across her, immovable, probably just about dead drunk before he made it to his last port of call. Ladylike to the last, she clutched the quilt about herself.

'You be crazy,' she hissed at me.

'Come with me,' I said, in spite of my saviour's alarm. 'Here's a chance for your dream to come true, for you to get away from here.'

'I can't,' she wailed. 'You don't know what they do to you when they catch you –'

Her wail hung in the air which went cold.

Three hooded figures had entered the room. Gurul, paralysed, stopped fighting off the boys. The other customers all paused in mid-punch, mid-gouge, mid-nasty-kick. You could hear the curlicues of hanging wall-plaster rustle on the chilled sweaty air.

Only one hood was back. Two faces were still in shadow under the hessian hoods, and the third face I found distinctly unlovable. Long and horselike as priests' so often are, shining with zeal as well as the stale shiny atmosphere, and with the bald eyelids and a very fleshy mouth which said, 'Whore-master. You are waited for.'

Gurul went that sick-bed colour the wanted man on the quay had gone.

He stepped out of the frozen tableau, towards the hooded robes.

The boys, about to go under when the tableau froze, came to life.

Miyak thrust a bundle into my arms.

30

'Cop tight,' he said. And as the priests led Gurul from the room, and the prostitutes and patrons began very slowly to decide to dare to look human again, and turn to each other to surmise, we ourselves became almost invisible. 'Now let's pass this rope round your shoulders,' the efficient boy with fists said. 'We're going to lower you out the window.'

'But I'll fall in the Canal –'

'No, it's covered in ice.'

'The ice won't bear our weight –'

'Well, anyway, there are lots of boats parked down there. Get in one. Wait for us.'

It was all I could do.

I let them sling me in a rope cradle under my armpits. We had an audience, which no longer tried to take any active part, still afraid almost to move, as though the hooded black-robes had left a pestilence in the room that mustn't be stirred. I held Seka very tight. I kissed her worried big-eyed look. I clambered over the window-sill as one boy held the window open.

Only then Shakina, the woman with the silver nails, screamed, 'Rubila! Eel! The new one's away!' and moved for the stairs.

'Don't worry about the rope giving,' a fair boy of sixteen told me. 'It's mine. I always carry it with me for emergencies – lassooing, or things.'

And luckily they couldn't bear to waste such an opportunity to use it.

They lowered me down, down, out in the icy air, down to the stink of the Canal.

I could hear the hullabaloo now up in the room. By now Eel, Lud and the doormen must have hurtled in with Rubila. And Rubila's customers would help. The boys would be done for.

I landed on ice. There was still rope to spare. Before I could give the rope a tug to say Stop lowering, it all snaked loosely down on top of me. Someone up there had let go.

I'd landed just in time. Now the ice was splitting, stars

31

shivering into existence in it as it cracked off in various directions.

I tried to hop to the nearest moored boat. The ice gave. My foot went through into water fiery-cold, and a scum of floating rubbish. I thought a swimming rat was nibbling my foot till I kicked at it and it turned bloated belly up. It had been drowned a long time before, and it was not a rat. It was a kitten.

I grabbed the boat and retrieved Seka who was slipping. I crouched in the dark boat.

If only there'd been less melodrama. If only the boys had been content to smuggle me out of the ground-level door, in someone's cloak, while Rubila wasn't looking.

Was it worthwhile waiting for the boys? They'd presently be slung out, covered in gore and glory, but then there'd be a search for me. Both Gurul and Rubila would have their bullies out combing the wharfs for me.

Or had the hooded priests by now chucked Gurul down some lovely religious oubliette for some lucky religious crimes?

A numb feel, or non-feel, spreading up me from my dripping icy foot, I eased out of the boat.

Two more hop-skips across crackly ice, and I was on shore. I turned down the street with Rubila's house of ill-fame on the corner.

It was a slimy smelly street. Not even one brazier lit it. This is the poorest-run City I've been in. Half the City hasn't even got street-lighting.

There was only one light below the stars. Halfway up the banked black sky a house-light, surely a home-light, beamed. It was bright and red – someone's home-fire. The City must rear like a hill over there. For want of anywhere else to make for, I made for that beaming little distant window.

Before I was halfway up the street, I heard the boys ejected from the building on the corner.

I paused. I looked back.

'And *stay* out – ' yelled Rubila's voice, not syrupy at all.

The boys, laughing and groaning, helped each other off the slippery cobbles.

'Girl! Girl!' they started calling.

I hurried back, hating their silly little guts.

'Here I am. Quiet.' I touched someone's cloak in the dark. He started nervously, then laughed.

'Here she is, Miyak. Here's your lost lamb.'

'However can I thank you all,' I cried, which just twenty-four hours before I'd been muttering fervently at Eel and his lot. I thanked them most rapidly, skimming over my words.

'Can we hurry?' I demanded. 'I'm sure they'll – '

And at this moment the doors opened again and men with torches ran out, and one torch came half the height of the others, which was Lud's.

'Come on,' the boys agreed.

*

We all made off silently. The boys were good at least at hugging the walls, and yet not tripping in the gutter. Of course they were just out of their apple-scrumping days.

Poor tiny Seka. This life I lead her, it's often almost a good thing she's dumb. Or perhaps by now the mite would have learnt to keep quiet anyway.

I'd been right about the hill.

Presently we were panting. The boys couldn't realise this really was life-and-death to me. A few hundred yards from our would-be pursuers, they relaxed. They began wheezing laughter. Their running slowed to a walk. They hit each other's backs great whacks of mutual congratulation.

'Did you see the old madam when she found we'd let the bird out of the cage in spite of her spurt up the stairs?'

'Did you notice that big one with the hairy chest?'

'Yes, he bashed me over the ear. I'll have a bruise like a plum tomorrow. Don't know what I'll tell Mum.'

'No, you nit, I didn't mean the bloke. The whore, the one I was with. In all the excitement I got away without paying her!'

Merry chortles. Womanhood outwitted!

33

'Well, lads, we'll have to find another brothel now.'

More merry chortles at this sophisticated remark. Lots of pretence at languid yawns. 'Oh, yes, dear old fellow, don't know how many houses of joy I've gone through. Always expelled, you know. Such a bore.'

Finally someone thought to take the baby from me. But she was so scared, I took her back though my arms ached.

I thought perhaps we were pretty safe now. We'd gone through so many arches, up so many side-twists.

I realised it wouldn't be such a labyrinth to a native, but also there were now other groups of late merry-makers. Some of them carried their own lanterns. Every now and then you could tell by the smell, a beggar emerged from some hole to suss us: a woman with a rag-bundle or a hook instead of an arm; a legless man bumping along in a wooden bowl brimming filth.

'Don't pickpockets have a marvellous time in this City after dark?' I said.

I realised I hadn't been so unexpectedly lucky as I'd thought, meeting a helpful group of over half-a-dozen boys. In fact, anyone who ventured out after sunset would be a fool (or desperate) to travel without several companions.

About twenty minutes later I realised there was grass underfoot. The houses, as far as I could tell in the blackness, had drawn apart.

'Are we out of the City?' I asked.

'No, but we're in the Suburbs,' they said.

Now there began to be light. We kept passing, near or far, different low banks of glowing red. Embers. Fires, banked, under control.

'Fires . . . ?' I said.

'Don't you know this City?' Miyak asked.

'I'm from Atlan,' I explained.

'Gosh,' he said. 'We must ask you all about that. Urga and Bronza will be so thrilled they'll be pissing themselves.'

Pause for appreciative laughter at his daring casual language.

'Well, you see,' he started again, 'this City opens out into sort of country in what we call the Suburbs. The houses are

34

in Circles, not Streets. And in the middle of each Circle there's a big green, where the well is, and where the women hang out their laundry to dry. And there's a big fire in each Circle.'

'Isn't that dangerous?'

'I suppose so,' he said vaguely. 'The houses are wood. Thatched. That's why we don't have braziers for street-lighting. But the fires are to roast the hunters' catch. It's traditional, even though there are butchers for the house-wives, as well as hunters now. Most of these fires have never had to be re-lit for generations. Even in rain the fire-watcher just puts a roof over.'

Steadily, as we climbed, the steady-flickery red light had been before us. It had been growing. As we emerged from each alley, tunnelled each deep arch, the light had grown. The embers of the fires waiting for the day to flame under the fire-watcher's faithful hand had not shone out from the hill as I stood in the sleazy street down by the Canal. But now that window-light I'd picked out was big and bright. Beaming. Beautiful.

Miyak opened a door below it.

'This is us,' he said, fitting the key back on his glass-chunky belt.

He guided me up the steps.

*

He yelled, 'Mother! Mothaaaa-aah!'

'Miyak! What is it, dearie?' a sharp voice immediately responded from upstairs.

'Come down, Mother! I've got something to show you!'

Instead of telling him to shut up his little surprises till morning, the woman's voice growled, 'I'm on my way.' The boys all grouped themselves on or round the kitchen table.

The stairs creaked so much I expected a very big Mother to come in. But though she was large, she was lean (and handsome). They must just be very creaky stairs.

'Have a nice evening, Miyak dear?' she said. 'Hello, you lot. Shall I fix you all a hot drink?' She was wearing an elaborate silky night-wrap, not very motherly, with the

35

deep swarthy split of her bosom showing, and for a moment of nightmare nonsense I thought I'd been tricked into yet another madam's house.

'Mother,' said Miyak, 'we came across this young lady and her poor little baby tonight. She has nowhere to stay.'

'And so?' said Mother.

'Well, I thought perhaps she could share the girls' room.'

Girls' room. Not again, I thought.

'No she could not!' Mother bellowed. 'What *do* you think this is? A doss-house?'

'She's cold and frightened.'

'She can shake and shiver in a cheap respectable Inn instead of trading on your good heart.'

'She's got no money –'

'It's all right, Miyak,' I cut him short. 'I'll go. Your Mother's quite right. I'll find somewhere.'

'And that pretty act won't get you my sympathy, either,' Mother snorted, handsome arms akimbo. 'You go, you go.'

'Mother – ' Miyak said. The other boys kept quiet, pushing pen-knives into the wood of the table, peacefully carving curly initials, on their faces the sort of looks that said, We know the score here, interference only makes matters tougher.

Besides, why should they really care? Any of them? They'd had their little adventure.

I couldn't immediately go out of the door, though I was hurrying out with my face burning and my head down over Seka.

Two girls came in. They stood in the doorway, paused in their talk to each other, staring at the big group in the fire-lit kitchen.

'Where, may I make bold to ask, have you tile-cats been out to till this ridiculous hour?' Mother inquired.

Still I couldn't get past them. They stood in the doorway.

'It looks as though Miyak's only just in,' said the fairer of the two – though that took some noticing. At first I thought it had been snowing, their hair was so light.

'It's different for Miyak,' Mother snapped. 'He's your brother. But you should have been in bed hours ago. I

36

thought you were. And *you* thought you'd sneak in with me in bed none the wiser. Well, now you're here, boil some hot milk all round. None for you – you're off to bed as soon as you're done.'

I made a move to the door as the girls stepped into the kitchen. A huge black hound, following them in out of the night, bared its fangs about the level of my thighs. I stopped.

'Who is this?' asked the girl with the hair like zinc alloy.

'Some stray Miyak brought,' Mother said. 'Get on with it.'

'Your girl-friend, Miyak?' asked the girl. 'Aren't you going to see her home at this time of night?'

'She has nowhere to go,' Miyak said uncomfortably.

'Then all the more reason to see her there,' the girl said. To me she said, 'Are you all right?'

'Your brother and his friends have just kindly got me out of a bad situation,' I said, not trusting myself to speak except very low. 'But I'll find a place to sleep.'

'You can sleep in our room,' this daffodil girl stated.

'Oh no she can't,' Mother said unequivocally. 'We don't know what she is, where she belongs. She may have fleas. The law may be interested in her.'

'And her baby may freeze tonight,' the other girl said.
Mother snorted.

'Babies don't freeze just like that. It's in a shawl.'

'Oh, well,' the daffodil-zinc-yellow girl said, 'it's true. We don't terribly want some beggar cluttering up our nice neat room. Why should we?'

'After all,' the snow-white one said, 'we're hardly some benevolent institution or something. Well, stranger, good luck.'

'Wait,' Mother snapped as I started to sidle past the dog which started a low reverberant growl in the bottomless pit of its throat. 'You, are you any good about the house?'

'Domestic service is my metier,' I said.

'If you make yourself useful we'll see about letting you stay a couple of nights,' Mother said. 'Girls, you'll make the best of it. This lady will stay in your room. Urga, put the milk over the fire. Bronza, go up and get some blankets

37

ready.'

'Ho, Mother,' the girl called Urga said in a whine. 'Why should we have some tramp in our room just because you decide to take pity on her?'

'I'll have no moaning from you,' Mother snapped.

The girl called Bronza went up the stairs behind the kitchen to prepare my bed. She winked at me.

'One of you boys, shut the door. There's ice on that draught,' the Mother said.

But Urga had to shut it. No one else would go near the dog which still stood by the door, its long eyes red.

*

The girls' bedroom was nice, yes. Not neat.

Bunks leaned groaning against one wooden wall. Blankets and rugs, and cushions instead of pillows (fervently giving up the ghost in a halo of little feathers whenever touched) had been laid for me on the matting floor.

An iron brazier hung on a rust-dark chain from a smoky rafter. Pink flames leapt in it. Little sparks sizzled, disappearing in mid-air.

'All up the slums-hill, I could see this window,' I said. 'I could see this fire. The window makes it blaze.'

Urga went across to pull the curtains. Disturbed on the window-jamb, a white slug paused perpendicular in its shiny ribbon of slime, eye-stalks alert. 'No light outside now,' Urga said. 'Still, we're snug eh?'

She tugged her long shapeless shift over her head. Naked but for a short woollen jerkin, she swung athletically on to the top bunk and sheathed herself between the holes of her tattered blankets.

'How recently were you both beaten up?' I asked the children. 'You're both covered in bruises.'

'And scabby knees,' Urga said. 'Good pickings.'

'We get beat up now and then.' Bronza coiled the ends of her hair – primrose more than daffodil or zinc I decided – into little bundles of old rag. 'But mainly it's just dashing round and bumping into things and falling off trees we're raiding and falling in streams we're jumping – you know.'

'Not really,' I answered. My own girlhood was very sedate, about five years ago when I was their age. Since my years with the nurses in the tall Tower, I've had a share of bruises – but never from my own choice.

Left to my own devices, I wouldn't have been energetic. 'And look at the boop.' Urga bent over my baby. 'Whuffling away, full of good hot milk and Mother's vile pasties.'

A voice is enough to disturb my baby. She jumped as though she had a tic and her eyes opened with a blind bloom on them but focused with a swift nervous effort. She saw me, which she doesn't always see on waking. She saw no sky passing, not even at a tranquil pace. She heard the children and I talking about nothing, busily. She sensed contentment for once, and I saw her mouth dimple to a contented smile. She still has suggestions of dimples.

The girls didn't ask much about me. I appreciated their discretion, and told them enough, without being asked.

My husband is fighting Gods know where, I said. The baby and I were put on a ship out of Atlan to safety. But the captain, though paid in advance for our passage, was not trustworthy. As soon as we docked here, we were sold on the waterfront, auctioned off. I told them the rest of the story in detail, and was lavish about their brother Miyak.

'You were very clever about getting your Mother to let me stay,' I said, hoping not to be tactless.

'Oh, anything she thinks we want, she vetoes,' said Urga.

'She hates us,' Bronza said.

*

Up the steps between the house-stilts with our dawn-collected firewood. The kitchen alive, awake now.

Fire blazing on the hearth. Porridge heaving and bubbling in a cauldron slung from the chimneypiece. Three sleek cats and numberless kittens purring at the flames or haughtily stalking invisible mice.

The saviour, the orange-haired boy Miyak on a stool in the chimney-corner, shaving chips of wood off a bow. Arrows stacked by.

Mother seated at the table, combing tangles out of the ginger hair of a little girl on her lap. The little girl poking chubby fingers (dimples instead of knuckles) into the stew on the table. A big man with a bristly fierce black beard hunched over the table, absently crumbling bread into his stew.

' 'Morning, people. 'Morning, Father,' sang the girls.

'This is our guest?' the man rumbled.

'By your leave,' I said.

He smiled at me, but his eyes wandered past me. He went on crumbling bread till his stew was crusted with it. Then he pushed it away untasted, said, 'Fit, my boy?' and strode out, grasping up a handful of javelins on his way. Two lean hounds followed him, keeping a respectful distance from Fernak.

Miyak jumped up to follow in his turn, dropped his bow, picked it up, went to the door, remembered he'd forgotten his arrows, went back for them, dropped his bow picking up his arrows.

'Aren't you going to kiss me Bye bye, Mi?' his Mother inquired.

Miyak sprang to his Mother, kissed her through the child's ginger curls, received a fat fistful of stew right beside his nose from the little sister, dabbed ineffectually at it, dropped his bow. Said Hello to me as he passed. Looked, in the morning, even more gallant, upright, and clean-living than last night. Odd I nearly slept with him last night – but if I had, overcoming my repugnance, I wouldn't be here now.

'Did you sleep well?' asked my new hostess-employer.

'Oh, *beautifully*,' I said.

She seemed taken off-guard by my enthusiasm. She poked fingers at Seka and offered to feed her. She told me to sit down and have breakfast before I helped the girls with the dishes, the rubbish-dumping, the bed-making and the day's laundry. I sat on a chair, got up, removed a kitten all bones and fluff and new from under the cushion, sat down again. I am part of the household.

PART TWO

# THE HOUSE ON STILTS

WE wash the dishes at the well in the middle of the green. The water freezes our fingers till we have to keep looking to make sure we've still got them. But all the other girls from the Circle come out at the same time, dish-washing time, with mops and cloths, and pull reputations to shreds and take turns pumping the bucket up and down.

The household laundry we can do with water boiled in the giant copper over the fire. It takes so long to boil, though, nearly all morning. Our hands are red and raw.

Meanwhile we've pummelled the household beds into shape. Shaken the pillows till the feathers fly.

Fed the fancy fish in Miyak's glass bowl. Changed their water, usually forgetting to do that first.

Laid meat and milk for the cats. Crumbs on the sills for the birds.

Hung the washing to flap in the wind.

Peeled the vegetables. Carried the rubbish to the fire which smells once you approach it out there on the green.

Seen it's raining. Dashed out to grab in the washing. Mouths full of pegs, arms of damp linen.

Scrub the kitchen floor.

Hunters home. Spits set up over the fire on the twilight green. All the Circle families out with carving-knives for the best cut of what their man got. The butchers all along with their baskets, chaffering with the hunters. Coins spinning in the gold light. First blood, then fat dripping, crackling roasting, and the spit-boys dancing in the grease.

Evening meal at the long table under the rafter-slung braziers.

The girls' friends, Miyak's boys, in to lie on their stomachs on the kitchen matting amongst feet and paws.

41

Talking, bickering, sewing, carving old wood. And maybe a cosy visit from the Temple bureaucrats, armed with 'correctors', who drop in at unexpected intervals to strip Father and make sure he's wearing the hair-shirt the Temple sentenced him to wear for a half-year to expiate his sin of forgetting his tax to the Temple on the cabbages he grows for the harvest-sacrifice. These men make it clear they like to be treated, as friends, to a chatty glass of wine after the forced stripping.

Good-byes at the door and the draught tearing the hinges.

Turns at the kitchen copper, stripping and sousing in the warmish water. First Miyak and Father, who emerge towelling and spluttering, and then we're allowed in to use the already scummy water – unpleasant if Miyak's decided to shave. But no time to boil more water, and that's the only pot that holds enough.

Bed. Curtains drawn against the creaking boughs, the howling rains, the winds, the Winter, the teeming slums. And any stray memories.

*

Living leisurely. Don't have to get anywhere before Snow. Or before Spring.

When I put a hand in my pocket there's always a nice fresh hanky there. In Winter, that may not be luxury. But it's contentment.

*

Sometimes I think, sort of haunted, of poor little Whatsername, the ladylike little tart still at Rubila's House, yearning for her rightful respectability and scared stiff to go out and find it. Still, what can I do except wish her well?

*

My hair has grown nearly right again, through the striped stage. My eyebrows are all right at last, too. Mother says I look a different girl and she'd never have made quite such

42

a fuss if she'd known that wasn't the real me. (She still doesn't know Miyak found me in a brothel, nor that any-one ever could find Miyak in one.) Father still looks through me, which now that I look presentable I am no longer grateful for.

*

The Winter is now so cruel that it must presently be over. The search for fire-fuel takes up nearly all of every day.

Each little wood-scrape, thin boughs sleeping in the sky, is awake at its roots as all the neighbourhood girls in their dun and grey and scarlet cloaks crouch around noses to the ground snatching twigs from each other's path. The stable-men are actually charging good coin for dung to be burnt in the braziers.

The East wind is full of poison. We can hardly see after it has blown its steady venom into our eyes.

The steep lanes are not mud, but ice – which is scaring when coming down (digging boot-heels in hard) but really beastly when going up, sliding backwards with nothing to hold on to.

I have boots now. An old pair of Miyak's. A bit too big for me, but the surplus space stuffed up with rags keeps them snug.

It now seems incestuous to think once I might have lain back and let Miyak do with me what ever way it is the boy does. No. Not incestuous. I have lain with my born-brother. And that in the back of my mind is a glory as well as a terror. Miyak is just the way one thinks of a brother, callow and stumbling over his own feet and maybe able to set the girl next door simpering, but a pain in the neck to the girls in his own house.

Somewhere, on or under the earth, my own brother lies hearing the same howling night winds I hear. My brother is a warm pain in my heart. I don't think of him at all till quite suddenly, maybe waking in the womb of the night, I ache like a pining dying animal. And there for comfort is the vivid vision of Smahil's smile, the consciousness of his

43

arms around me as they last were and in an odd way always
will be.

\*

It's too cold to trudge through sludge to the pump. We tear
icicles from the eaves and boil them.

\*

'Our Army are past the marshes. They'll be in the City
tomorrow, after noon,' Miyak joyously cartwheeled into
the fire.

\*

A morning making ready for the Procession. The City is
delirious. The route of the Procession is being hung with
banners and ropes woven of flowers.

The Army has been away in the North over a year.

Well, well, what a terrible long time.

Returning are the flower of the City's manhood – soldiers, captains, and a young Prince who is the nephew of
the City's top brass.

Simply to be part of the crowd cheering, Urga and
Bronza (and Mother and Miyak) are taking as much care
as brides before the night.

They have washed their faces in the rain-water-butt outside the kitchen door. (Water like silk but cold enough to
break your veins and surfaced by drowned gnats and ship-
wrecked twigs.) They have poked sticks up the chimney
and drawn them down charred with soot to draw round
their excited eyes.

They have braided their pale hair, and stuck little flowers
in the plaits.

\*

The flowers twisted in ropes along the route soon broke and
scattered, in spite of the cordons of civil police straining
arms-linked before the crowd. It didn't seem an awful
shame – very big coarse shrub-flowers, mostly leaves, all
that could be got so early in the year except for tiny little

44

hedgerow and ditch flowers which would have taken years to weave into ropes.

The crowd was going mad. Plenty of people had been camping in vantage-points since yesterday. Pedlars with trays of sticky insect-haunted sweets, or sellers of 'hot' drinks were doing a roaring trade. The usual number of nits fainted away in the crush.

As usual, too, apparently, our family was late.

Mother prepared to stand quite resigned at the back of the crowd. But the girls craned their necks as they heard a boy call their names.

The voice added various insults about blind bats till Bronza cried, 'It's Ogdrud, up on the parapet above our heads!'

I'd swear both girls are virgin. They giggle at bed-time about boys, as about everything. If there were more to say, they'd say – they go into pungent details at times. They know as much as any children brought up with animals. But also they talk with wonder and ignorance – I mean, they even seem to think human beings never make it except in the same position as animals. So I'm sure this Ogdrud is not the lover of either girl. But they flutter about him. A dark flash-eyed lean muscular boy, a friend of their brother Miyak's, in fact the boy with the fists who first threatened my dark master Gurul.

Hanging dangerously off the parapet of an unfinished building, he jeered, 'What a view you have down there!'

'We're coming!' The girls, flushed, started scrambling.

'You'll do no such thing,' Mother turned on them. 'That building is Temple property. It's sacred.'

This is not only the dirtiest, but the most religion-bound City I've ever been in.

'Oh, go on, Mother, eh,' Miyak wheedled, coaxing head to one side, his diadem of glass jewels slipping. 'I know it's hardly decent for the girls. But for *me* – '

And the girls sprang up the scaffolding like mountain goats, not that I've seen mountain goats on scaffolding, as Mother simpered permission.

I wasn't thrilled about seeing some little alien Army pass.

45

Going by the City's general state of prosperity, I expected its Army to be a parochial raggle-taggle goose-stepping to a blare of pompous bands. But with Mother so unusually cowed, I followed up the scaffolding.

And suddenly Miyak was seized by big scruffy men all in black.

We hardly looked. Everybody was jostling everybody else. Most Processions I've watched from the refrigeration of marble balconies, slaves around me genteelly crooking their little fingers as they tossed rose petals on whichever hero I indicated. In spite of the smells and spitting of *this* crowd, I didn't at all mind the warmth it generated even in this freezing air. The jostling and roughness were part of it all. But quite without warning that had become serious. Ahead of us, above us, Miyak cried out.

The big men were dragging him. They weren't gowned and hooded, but they were so greasy and unsavoury that I knew at once they had something to do with the Temple.

Miyak, vainly trying to get his hand to his rusty little dagger, was being hauled off to our left.

'What's the boy done?' I shouted, making a diagonal dash across a shaky ladder in order to block their way.

'This is Temple property,' the biggest stolidly echoed Mother's words.

'But we're on it – others are on it – why not arrest us all?'

'He is desecrating Temple property by using it to sightsee off of.' The man, like all officials, couldn't answer a question except with a rule from the book.

'Come on, then,' I said as the sisters arrived beside me. 'Arrest us all. We're all guilty.'

'He's to be made example of. The master pointed just him out, the one with orange hair.'

'The master? A priest?'

The man was tired of my catechism. He swiped out with one black-gloved hand. His glove was banded in iron. I fell aside.

The sisters half-steadied me against the ladder. Miyak was gone.

'Where have they taken him?'

46

'We must follow and put the mistake right before Mother finds out – ' Urga said.

'Mistake?' Bronza said. 'No mistake. They weren't making any example. They didn't care who missed seeing him hauled off, nor who stayed. Someone wanted him got rid of.'

'Got rid of . . . ?'

'They went off there, through that sort of arch.'

With one accord, the three of us swung off in the same direction. It would have taken too long now to call Ogdrud through the press. Even now, the crowd was so thick and reluctant to budge an inch either way, we might have lost the trail. I wished the girls' dog Fernak were with us – since they told me how Father brought him home as a snarling pup, I've known he is a wolf, made motherless by the Hunters' arrows and sentimentally adopted by Father into his ignorant household as a taciturn 'dog'.

The big half-finished building (thronged with spectators) was rough-hewn from sandstone interlaid with blocks of granite dull-gleaming as Winter itself, spider-webbed by scaffolding and dangles of rope ladder for the masons and carpenters.

We dashed and dodged. Where we couldn't push our way, we applied a sharp elbow or even used our nails. And were off again before we could be apprehended.

With the blare of brass I'd expected, the returning Army hove into hearing. The crowd raised a roar and began waving like a forest about to crash on its face.

*

I thought the wind was blowing fresh rain against my face. Ages later I bothered to put up my hand, and it was later again that I glanced at my hand and realised it was red, that the man's glove had cut my cheekbone.

We were following a sort of tunnel, or open gallery. It was easy enough where it was walled in from the open sky. But where it widened out and provided a view of the City below, we had to thrust our way through the belligerent crowd.

Now and then, at some turning ahead, we'd see the flutter on the raw wind of Miyak's cloak flanked by the grim black gaolers, or the flash of his red head which had called down on him the attention of some ill-wisher.

We could guess the route of the Procession for a long way, before we saw it, by the cheering of the crowds in the winding City ways. Finally it spear-headed in sight, slow, like a conjuring trick.

First of course, catching from below the corners of our eyes even in our panic, came the routine girls, scattering the routine flower petals. Their deep baskets were still just about full. Obviously they had been told to scatter sparingly so as not to run out of flowers. They were scantily-dressed, poor creatures, sand-papery with goose-pimples in spite of the Winter sun, but the police must nearly have burst blood-vessels restraining the crowd.

Now the returning regiments.

Fascinating as waves always at a shore. All these men, beautiful as only soldiers can be. All those buckles and buttons and belts and boots. High shakos with rakish peaks under which you could just get the glitter of male eyes which have beheld battle and all the rest of it. Straps biting chins already harsh with stubble since the morning's parade shave. Thousands and thousands of epaulettes shivering. Thousands of military shoulders.

Now we could hardly shove our way. But it was a consolation that neither could the black brutes ahead of us. We were becalmed, forced to watch above the multitude.

Just as you are bored by the ranks of scarlet and gold, a space. Just the road and the petals trampled into the dung.

And then perhaps a strutting corporal with a mascot, a young pacing puma on a stiff taut studded leash blazing with emeralds like his eyes.

And the ranks of black and crimson, and the tassels' swishing mirrored in the boots glossy as black glue. And the crowd holds its breath in delight to hear the marching boots and the hissing, as of snakes passing, of thousands of tassels.

And then the blare of another band, accompanied by

small boys cartwheeling and strumming twangy ghirzas. And then the roar of the crowd redoubled, and the heroes on horses.

'Here's the big brass,' the girl Urga says, meaning not the band but the top men on story-book stallions.

All the weak sun, magnified, shimmering, shining, spitting, glowing, glittering and dizzying off swords and daggers and studs and straps. And now not just steel but jewels below us.

'Our Prince, our Prince!' a large youth beside us yelled as the crowd started to dance up and down, having no room to move any other way.

'Ugly-looking git,' commented Bronza.

'Cor! Who's that?' Urga's breath blossomed blue.

'Who?'

'The one in pale leather – the one with our Prince?'

'Oh, he's some Major in the Northern Army,' our neighbour said.

'Then why's he returning with ours?'

'He's in charge of a Northern battalion, four heavy-strength companies sent by them to "help out" – or keep an eye on us, in other words. He was born here, anyway, he's a nobleman of this City who went off and joined them.'

'He's – oh, he's – ' Urga said.

'He's not all that,' the youth sneered.

I tried to identify in the mass below the men they meant.

I realised which must be their Prince. That big beetle-browed boy on a thoroughbred pinkish-beige mule as shambling as himself. An idiot Prince? No, I didn't think so. There was a steady gleam of stubborn watchfulness in the small eyes black and deep-set under the low brows. He was dressed not very royally, more like a monk, not in a military uniform either, just in a plain tunic in a plain dark colour with dandruff on the shoulders. Navy stubble shadowed his jaw. One of those two-shaves-a-day men.

Before I could pick out the man who'd excited Urga, we were on the move again.

Miyak had been dragged through a loophole in the crowd. Forcing our own way, we found ourselves on a flight of steps leading downwards at a nasty rapid pace. They weren't proper steps, just haphazard cuts for the workmen's feet in the rock. The crowd thinned. The tunnel turned. There were hairpin bends, steep. 'We'll end breaking our necks,' I said.

We stopped. A carillon of shiny chill sunlight met us, and set my cut smarting. We had emerged at street level.

Here was one of those breaks in the Procession. The road lay empty, one band disappearing to our left, another advancing some way to our right.

Straight ahead of us, the black men gripped Miyak across the empty road. Miyak's legs looked dispirited and spindly.

Urga began to dash across in pursuit. 'Wait – ' I cried as the next segment of Procession bore down on us. 'You don't know what they'll use him for!' she cried. But she was just too late. The battalion was on us. And the mascot, a mountain-lion as tall as a heifer with muscles like polished orichalc gone molten, restive on its leash only just kept taut by its trainer, decided to spring at this distraction in its path.

Urga, like a child's toy of two dimensions, folded to the road at once.

The puma lowered itself splendidly above her. It took its time, for you could see the sweet articulation of the golden glory of its muscles, yet it was so swift its trainer stood paralysed. Then he honked some word, its name perhaps. But the command was lost in the deep *Oooohh*, the thrill of the watching crowd at this lovely development.

I thought I heard the crunch of Urga's thigh-bone. I saw the deep carnivorous rose opening of the puma's throat.

Nobody had ordered the soldiers to halt, so they didn't. The boots and the tassels kept on coming, coming, swishing. Lifting and beating the ice particles of the road, I thought they'd continue right on and over the collapsed child and the feeding growling glory.

The trainer barked command after command and jerked on the studded leash. The puma was young and half-wild anyway. It simply lifted its head and showed its teeth at him

50

and the sun skittered off the teeth and Urga lay with her face white and her eyes closed ready for their last closing and her ashy hair in the dung.

Then there were immense claws on the road beside the child's hair. And the man, who'd been riding on the huge piebald Northern bird beside the Prince, had spurred ahead and come up by the out-of-control mascot.

'Fool!' he barked at the trainer, only he used a worse word, and impatiently his sword was out and it was a dart of pure poison at the animal's great throat, the flash turned the creature and spun it over and it gave a marvellous gurgle and the blood came.

The killer-rider left the trainer to help the girl from the road that had nearly been her grave and was the beast's. But the trainer gaped at the rider and it was Bronza who raced to lift her sister's head.

'The beast cost solid gold from the hill tribes, sir – ' expostulated the trainer.

'I'd've pinked your throat too if there'd been time,' curtly said the rider. 'Don't you know better than to let a beast's price stop it ruining a City's Procession of peace?'

He turned back to his place in the line and the marching boots marched past us. He hadn't cast a glance at the face of the girl he'd saved, not even to see whether she were alive. But I'd seen his.

Sharp face under a shako. A foxy or ferret-sharp face – narrow pale unreliable eyes, a straight blunt nose and jaw, and a narrow pale mouth – Gods I wanted to shout Ihavekissedthatmouthathousandtimes!

I didn't recognise him! I didn't recognise him! My mouth went dry. Now passed away from us on into the Procession and cheering crowd, the foreign Major in the flashy uniform was my brother, Smahil, my lover, the father of my lost son.

*

Painfully I pieced together the evidence. The sisters and I wearily climbed the hill to the Temple outside the City. I stared the sky out.

Urga was not hurt. 'No skin broken,' she said, though Bronza had to support her because she was shaky. But, 'There's only the Temple left,' they said, 'and we mustn't waste any more time. We can't go back and tell Mother he's gone – we must at least be able to tell her where, *why*.'

Personally I had no hope that we should find a clue of the boy's fate. He'd be an anonymous entry in the book of the Officially Forgotten. I dared not guess, for my conscience' sake, what he'd done to incur official wrath – nor whose official wrath. I simply knew the man Gurul, from whom Miyak half-cavorting had wrested property, had noted the boy's distinctive colouring and would have been looking out for it on any public day – and was in cahoots with the Temple.

The clouds piled up and the City spread below us.

This is the City I was born in. This is the little dictatorship ruled by my Mother.

I *have* come home.

Or I have, in a sense, come to the only place I can call home – the City in which I was brought up, born, bred from long lines of chill-ambitioned ancestors. No wonder I didn't recognise it. I've seen the City itself twice only, though I lived my first seventeen years here. Once, from the carriage in which I rode on a troubled drum-hearted evening, with my Mother and the wife-witch Ooldra, from the nurses and nursery-Tower of my childhood to the enemy campment where I was to seduce and kill the Northern dragon-General who had demanded me as hostage.

That awful evening. We had passed Canals and slittish windows all in a storm darkness. The storm had gathered from the North, the South, the East. I had passed away into it. It had closed. It had gathered me in, in and closed me to its black dark heart.

I had visited the City and my Tower again.

I had been the General's bride, and he the new Emperor of North and South and Atlantis-across-the-Ocean. The City had been any City to a visiting conqueror, sheeted in flags, drifted in petals, misted in wine.

I had not recognised it, not this third bitter time. I had thought it the poorest nastiest way ever I'd entered a city, at filthy wharves and a Canal-quarter that was a sprawl of slums. But in a creeper-crawling log house on stilts in a small friendly swamp, my City had welcomed me, home.

*

Seka's grandmother is my Mother. My Mother is ruling this City. I have but to ask. They would tell me where the palace is. I have only to find the way to the big bloated building.

'Mother!' I would say. 'It is I!'

The marble would echo, 'Cija!' The slaves, the soldiers would shout, 'Cija!'

My Mother would be brisk with pleasure.

Behind the pleasure there would be a sort of paroxysm, an ecstasy.

'Cija, you're back with me, child!' she'd say, madly busy arranging banquets in my honour. 'What have you done to leave your husband? What are you thinking of to leave him? We must get him over here.'

'Don't tell him I'm here,' I'd plead but she'd tell him.

She'd bring him over. She needs him. She loves and hates – not him, but his name and his might and his Armies. She loathes him because he and his father before him destroyed her land, this little land. She loves him because of all men it is he she needs, his Armies which can keep her dictatorship safe from the threats which tower over it from all sides.

She'd pay no attention to what I wanted, pay no attention to *me* at all. I'd be a pawn again. I'd be the wife of the General again, drowning in a purple political sea.

Now I am Cija. I am a stranger-woman, peeling vegetables and poking fires for my supper at a house-woman's charity, and at this very moment climbing a cold shiny hill to the tomb-like Temple of my father's religion, but if I die it will be because of a little chance directly concerned with me, not with the pawn labelled *General's Wife*.

I shall not ask the way to the palace, in case at some limpid hour I might find my feet wandering that way.

*

On a hill, the Temple.

By the time you have crawled up the winding mud road, you are exhausted already. You are panting dry-tonsilled. They allow roast-acorn sellers by the gates as long as three-quarters of the trade profit goes to the Temple.

Normally it is a quiet place pushing sky.

The walls are all of terribly old rock crystal. Broad and squat in proportion to its height, the Temple crouches like a giant frog's jelly-sac, and the little embryo dots inside it are the room-divisions, the hanging lamps and the altars. You can't go to worship in peace, and scratch your ear or pick your nose, without feeling the action observed for miles around.

Of course, that's perhaps the way a Temple should be. No privacy: a reminder that We Are Ever Watched.

As you enter the gates, the heads look down on you from their pikes.

Heads embalmed to last indefinitely in their indefinite glory, till the vu'tures and hawks, and the corrosive rains, have discovered them. Some are still perfect: some, white skulls with shreds of flesh or hair clinging, or with one glazed sad martyr's eyeball left in a bone socket.

These are the saviours – the sacrifices, the men and women who have been picked out by lot in past decades of threat or flood or famine, and died by the priest's knife that the fates might be appeased.

My husband has been responsible for most of the recent heads. And I was another sacrifice to appease him.

Now they moulder in honour in the blue air. Some wear garlands of withered flowers, which from time to time are tossed up there by the children training for priesthood in the school attached to the Temple, who enjoy aiming and competing to see how many sacred skulls they can lasso with garlands.

'Always remember,' Mother murmurs as she passes

under these relics, 'that no matter how bad things are, they might yet have been worse but for those human beings.'

In spite of the embalming fluid, a faint odour of decay hangs about the gates, which must be worse up higher. Down by the ground, filtered by the still and holy air, it is not unpleasant — just awesome, a little acrid, a little sweet, reminding one of the worm that waits us all and the Fate that watches us all and the god/demon forces that pull us all.

But in this horrible hour of Thanksgiving, nothing was quiet and nothing seemed holy. The road, the gates, the Temple, all were crowded with sweating citizens. There were queues to sign names, and bribes to officials to tick unsigned names. The chanting never stopped and the courtyard doves had flown away.

*

Everyone registered in the City annals must attend the evening Thanksgiving service at least once a fortnight, or their names will be struck off the list of official citizens unless they are under twelve years of age. This means that all the respectable folk, Suburbia must attend. The slums don't register their names anyway. And nobility can attend in its private chapels. (In other words, pull private strings to get its names ticked off.)

'What is the Thanksgiving for?' I once asked.

Tonight, for returning our big soldiers to us. But always for something. For our well-run City, for the Gates which somehow (haphazardly) kept at bay the pestilences running riot in the lower reaches of the City, for our shining gliding Canals (which more than anything spread the pestilences) and most of all, always, for our chanting priesthood eternally interceding between our sins and our Gods.

'These people should be at home.' I watched two children leading a thin bent cripple, a girl no more than twenty, whose rags brushed back in the wind and showed her sparrow thigh. 'We'll be bronchitic by evening.'

'Better lose your life than your immortal soul, as Mother says.'

'She doesn't mean a word of it. She just likes seeing what the neighbours decided to wear,' Bronza whispered, puffing blue breath into her hands to keep them awake.

But there must have been some such fear laid on the crowd. Or why in this weather, and after the strain of the Procession, was it so vast? No soldiers, no sun here.

'Do you know a priest who can tell us what they've done with Miyak?' I whispered.

'No one *knows* our priests,' they answered.

In this transparent envelope of frog-spawn, we heaved our shoulders against our neighbours'. Hate and resentment glowered from every face as our voices rose in the chants of praise and gratitude. No sun beamed in on us. But we perspired.

*

I was black and blue by the time we had settled into the crowd. At every step the unappetising scarecrows that pass for men here thrust their leering faces before mine. In a nearby corner of the space, there was shouting round an impromptu cockfight: just as a knife-fight broke, because the owner of the losing cock swore there was poison on the winner's spur, deep heart-stopping gongs sounded to silence us all.

The Temple hall seemed paved by all the crackly stale ice which had been tramped in by continuous congregations. In the distance, raised on a dais but still nearly invisible, a little white figure waved its arms and yelled for an hour in a little crackly stale voice.

'Do you love him,' I asked, 'or fear him, that you turn out in such cold?'

'He is the priest,' Urga said uncomfortably. 'He can curse, you know. And levitate.'

'All done with mirrors,' I said sardonically.

'I know you're travelled and experienced, Cija, but even though our Dictatress imprisoned him recently for inciting rebellion against her, he had to be released because of the outcry and the Curses his priests put on us all – he really

56

is a perilous old man,' Bronza muttered into her handclasp of breath.

He led the chant, he tossed our names in the tripod flame. I strained to see his face. He was too far away to be more than a white rod. Yet this is the man who fathered me on my Mother the Dictatress, and fathered my brother Smahil on the wife-witch Ooldra.

The evening deepened.

And deepened. Stars stabbed the roof. The waiting crowd murmured, though they hardly dared even that with the priest's gimlet eye and supra-awareness in the same oxygen.

'We must get out of the congregation. Must find Miyak – before it's too late,' I urged them.

'Not now. Not safe. Later, when the first service disperses. We can get behind-scenes in the confusion.'

'It is night,' Urga groaned, leaning heavily on me – we were taking it in turns to lean on each other. Around us arm-cradled children were snoring gruffly, and women slept still chanting on their husbands' shoulders.

About an hour later, two more white figures arrived on the platform with gongs. They struck them. A thin *buhm* trailed over the waiting crowd, who raised a shout that would have been ear-splitting if not so ragged.

'The evening Festival is over.'

'Well, it was most festive.' I turned.

The congregation stirred. It came almost painfully to life. Many were too stiff to walk, too hoarse to curse or plead, for a way through the inrushing mass who'd been waiting in the courtyard for the next service.

'What happened?' asked the newcomers, who at least had been allowed to sit while waiting.

'Some fool of a priest boozed on his evening wine forgot the gong,' a man near us answered through swollen lips.

'Hush,' others hissed in panic, for Temple wine is the symbol of sacrificial blood.

At this moment the sky split in two. It stayed green as silver for a whole minute. The forked snake-tongue of

57

lightning hit the earth with a double crack that vibrated every vein there.

'GodsparemethatIsinned!' a woman shrieked and would have cast herself to the ground but that the crowd was too thick and too panicky. We recognised her as Mother. We would have left her, without discovering ourselves to her, but she saw us and shrilled, 'So here you are? Where's Miyak then?'

The sky came black. A peal of thunder went rumbling twice round the sky, mighty echoes throwing others back. The sound made one realise what a large sky is up there.

'Flee!' Mother ululated.

We got her running in the right direction.

A man white-faced in the surging crowd overtook us.

'Where the lightning struck, a woman was killed!' he shouted. 'Her hair exploded in a sheet of flame!'

'It was the red-haired Goodwife of the 8th Circle!'

'She was no Goodwife!' Mother cried. 'I happen to know who she was carrying on with. It's a judgement! The priest took the opportunity of showing he knew! You can't hide ought from him!'

Now we were out of the Temple. Raindrops fell on us with the force of hailstones, straight down on us, no wind. But Mother had cheered up.

'Fine,' Urga said with the insensitivity of the young. 'If that adulteress hadn't been struck, Mother would have sworn you called the storm down with your ceaseless mockery. Thrown you out in it.'

'I hope your Mother never finds out where I was found,' I said in a low voice. And then – 'Do you see that man in the crowd?'

What's more, Gurul had seen me.

'That man is my master,' I said.

So quickly even I hardly noticed, we ducked under a drenched straw wall-curtain depicting holy geometric abracadabra. We pushed through a little door, and stood panting rather in a cold opaque passage. A pattern of doors led off its sides. Without hesitation the sisters chose the fourth on the left. Now we were in a courtyard with very high walls that showed only a ceiling of gathering storm. The raindrops, huge and heavy as they were, were so wide-spaced one hardly noted them.

'What's that sound?' I asked.

'From below,' they said briefly. 'The prisoners.'

Half-muffled, half magnified by the stone, a rise and fall, like the belling of hounds, till one heard the tangible despair in the notes, the whimpering and the pain and the prayer.

And a constant rumbling whirring, as of vast machines, manufacturing instant constant-pain.

Past two gates. The sisters knew how to twist the air-locks beside the skeletons hung manacled where they had starved – yet other sacrifices, honoured with chanting all the slow days of their death.

Through a narrow cloister fringed by the storm-slashed splash of fountains. Presently a bigger place – half-room, half-courtyard, for its roof lay partly open to the stars glittering and skittering through the vast ragged clouds.

Now both the silver sister and the primrose sister appeared silver.

'Relax now,' Urga said, quite loudly. 'No pimp knows these religious mazes.'

Instantly, at her voice, the paving round us shot up in bumps.

'Urga! Bronza!' hushed a chorus. Dozens of children's voices. These bumps were the Temple pupils, sitting up in their blankets, darting in their white-fleece nightgowns off their mattresses.

'This is their dormitory,' Bronza said.

'Why are you here?' they cried in delight. 'Can we have an adventure?'

'They infiltrate everywhere, these children,' Bronza said to me as Urga knelt among the children and began talking rapidly.

'They'll know whether a new prisoner arrived today, and where he's been stowed. They may not know, though, for what fate. We teach here now and then – not very successfully, though it brings in pocket-coin. We can read *and* write, you know. But whenever the children get restless, they start screaming, *Look, the walls are collapsing* and all start running out.'

'You're fooled?' I asked to keep her mind off Miyak.

'It always *might* be true,' carelessly said Bronza. 'In their schoolroom a corner of the ancient masonry is pushed – one corner-stone actually lifted – by the centuries' growth of a tree with roots gripping the stone. Often you see new cracks spread.'

Meanwhile Urga was explaining to the children about our starlight visitation. She was alarmingly truthful.

'We were chased by a man of evil,' she said with some relish. 'We had to use your dormitory as sanctuary.'

The children were not alarmed. 'Let's go and find him and lead him a dance till he's lost in the vaults,' they suggested.

At this moment, lights dizzied into the dormitory. Gurul had found us after all. With him were three men swinging torches spattering sparks.

'How – ?' Urga angrily demanded as she grabbed me and set off running again. 'He must be pretty well in with Temple secrets.'

'Hey!' Bronza whistled a sharp odd whistle. 'This man is the man of evil!'

The children whirled and scattered. They ran this way and that, flapping their fleece gowns and fur sheets, setting in seesaw motion the great glacier-like models of the world, sculpted in ground glass to show the earth's innards and the sub-strata levels that lead to the eternal fires – the cursing dodging men dared not touch for these are sacred children who will one day be priests with power not only over life and death but beyond.

Urga and Bronza hurled with me into a narrower darker passage than yet we'd been in. Our steps echoed and the roof was very low – I banged my head and saw colours whirligig in the dark.

'We're underground,' they panted. 'This leads right under the hill. It comes up under the Palace itself. But we've never been that far. With luck we'll calculate right,

60

and come up under the outskirts of the 7th Green.'

'How can you calculate right? We've no light!'

'The different turnings smell different, and echo different from each other.'

'What if Gurul traps us down here?'

'We can always elude him,' the fearless little sisters panted. Elude him, elude him, laughed the echoes running the swift passages.

Presently the echoes were joined by another sound, a pealing clangour, repeated and repeated.

'The children have set off their alarm bell,' Urga said.

'I'm glad they waited till we were out of the way, or we could end in severe ghastly trouble, found in these holy places at night. I bet the pimp lands in it up to his nose.'

'Have the children no guards actually in their room?'

'No. They would be mortal guards and would contaminate the children's sleep. Their dreams must be undisturbed by anything but the natural elements and the moans of the Religious-prisoners from down below, and recorded next morning by meticulous scribes in case there's anything of import to the nation in them. But the secret locks on the doors and the skeletons of the Long Death and the spiked walls should be enough protection. I can't imagine how the men got in.'

Now a red glow tongued along the passage behind us. We could see each other's expressions – and there behind us stretched the angry red flicker.

'Fire?'

'Sweet Gods.' Bronza stopped in her flight and whispered in awed horror. 'The sparks from the thugs' torches must have set light to the children's beds!'

'But it's all stone,' Urga comforted. 'There's no wood, no dangerous thatch like our Greens.'

'There are plants and creepers –'

'All be sopping with storm.'

Nevertheless the glow pursued us, and a gusty sound like a distant sea grown savage, and a smell acrid as the heads on the gateposts but less sweet.

61

'Have to turn off here,' Bronza gasped as the heat became intense.

And we right-angled into an amazing passage, which the flaring light showed us was tiled intricately with chips of enamel and strips of gilt.

'Can you hear flames?' I asked. 'That gargling sound?'

'Gosh oh gosh,' the sisters remarked in a most upset way. 'Keep to the centre along here.'

'Why? What's at the sides?'

'The fire would be better than this –'

'For pity's sake enlighten me,' I felt almost amused by my exasperation.

Urga explained, 'There are wire-netting fences either side of us, and behind them are fairly wide streams, stocked with alligator.'

'And we're a bit anxious in case the netting is thin at any point, or broken – in this dark we wouldn't know till too late.'

Now my amusement vanished like a blown candle to be replaced by a pitchy pit of blackness. The sounds took on significance. Splashes, and barks with a gurgling quality. Long tails threshing in liquid darkness.

'What are the beasts guarding?' I asked.

At this very instant a flare sprang up in front of us. I saw everything suddenly. The gilt glitter on the walls. The little sisters cowering unusually. The green water, full of eyes, tails, jaws, scales. And in front of us, holding high their torches, the whore-master Gurul and his three thugs.

'Admit that we're efficient trappers,' Gurul said.

'How do *you* know your way in these walks?' Urga demanded, in fact accused.

'You're fairly proficient yourselves,' Gurul remarked. 'Little tunnel-explorers, little pale worms, is what we have here, boys.'

'Worms get thrown to alligators,' one of the men drawled. I couldn't see his face past his torch, but he sounded kinky.

'But one of these worms,' Gurul said, 'is too rich a maggot for the beasts. And I think we'll have other uses for the extra two. Commercial uses, and of course pleasure before commerce, lads, that's your due. Your bonus, that is. No one will know that these silly children did not simply lose themselves in their exploring. No one will know, a year from now, whether they are not still wandering in the labyrinths they so girlishly delighted in. Alligators don't bear witness.'

Suddenly Bronza had sprung forward as her own dog would have done if only he'd been here. She knocked the torch from one man's hand. It fell and rolled, past the netting. The alligators bayed as it struck the water and was extinguished.

Instantly Urga and I followed example. But we were not strong enough. We were easily tossed aside. The netting rattled. The alligators were alert. They sensed their own possible profit.

'Leave the girls,' I said. 'You have me now. Your coins are re-won, your pride is satisfied.'

'Ah, you're a move of the game behind me,' Gurul blandly assured me. 'When I bought you on the quay, ragged starving slut you were, you didn't tell me there were those in higher places ready to barter double, treble, quadruple for you.'

'What does he mean?' said Urga irrepressibly inquisitive.

'Word has reached the Temple of your apparition in our land,' Gurul said, watching me closely.

Who had seen me? Who had recognised me? Who had had swift malice to tell my father? Now I knew my fate sealed. If this dark man is a spy of my father's, I am done for. My father has always wanted me dead. For my parentage to be known would mean his dissolution in the eyes of the people. A High Priest must be celibate. If both I and my mother vouched for his fatherhood, the people would doubt him. And now, too, I am the Emperor's wife, estranged wife maybe, but nevertheless my husband is ally to my mother, because she has consented to rule this country in trust for him as his regent in return for his powerful protection; and an ally of my mother is a threat to my father who is her devoted avid enemy.

'You are going to kill me,' I said flatly.

'That's not our decision,' he said. 'But we're taking you to someone who will decide soon enough.' And they seized my arms.

I struggled. The netting rattled, clanging. The alligators, aroused, lashed the water in a frenzy as they crowded to the netting, jaws agape. They started a chorus of encouraging barks and roars, urging the men to feed us to them.

A shaft of green light smote into the flame-flare and one woman strode amidst us from a new opening in the wall-bend ahead of us.

The men drew aside. One shielded his face. Gurul bowed his head.

'You are disturbing my animals,' the woman said in a low voice you had to strain your ears to catch.

I couldn't have shielded my face. I couldn't take my stare off her. She was naked, yet clothed from head to foot. Her hood, her sleeves, her trousers with feet on them like tights, were all one piece. Even her face was covered – yet this whole covering was transparent, a filmy big-pored gauze. Only her long-nailed fingers were entirely bare, pointing out from the gauze mitten-ends of her garment. Through this floss, this fabric fog, her eyes and teeth and nipples and navel glared. The gauze was covered with sparkle inside and out – sewn with chips of crystal, little lines of adhesive rhinestone tattooing her breasts, a flash of mirror in her restless navel. You couldn't see her hair, it was stiff with plaited gold. She had gold teeth and long gold eyes and as her nostrils flared in anger a gold stud blinked in each of the small dark caverns.

'We have had to take captives on the High Priest's business. Now we shall leave your creatures in peace,' Gurul said, omitting to address her by any title. He spoke, however, with extremely grave reverence, in fact with a certain fear. I believed her name must be too dread to mention aloud.

'There is no capture in my animals' corridors that is not capture for them,' the same low voice said.

'With all respect, we cannot give these maidens to your

64

animals,' Gurul said. 'They are expressly ordered for the High Priest.'

'These corridors are my animals', and belong to no priests,' the woman rustled.

'We will throw the two fair ones to your animals,' Gurul sacrificed his profit, 'if we can reserve the other for our Master.'

'Here, my animals are your Masters.'

There was no argument from any of them. They could hardly look at her. They stood limply. Their torches smoked.

'The two fair ones are yours, Lady,' Gurul said, gabbling the *Lady* very quick in case it were wrong, yet not daring to use her name or true title.

'Then throw them in,' the woman said.

Relieved, their tension slackened, the men bundled the sisters up in their arms. Urga and Bronza both started to scream as they saw the edge of the netting rise to meet them, then veer away beneath them. They scratched and scraped at the netting and their captors' arms, and kicked violently backwards with their whole bodies. The waiting alligators threshed the water to a boiling cauldron.

The alligators couldn't wait. They started rearing. Their soft pale under-bellies glowed.

The biggest, a nightmare male, caught in his teeth the sleeve of the man hefting Urga.

The grinning greedy brute would not let go. That was all. Simply, and by this single inexorable logic, it pulled the man shrieking up and against and up and over the netting. The sleeve tore as the man struggled, but by now the monster's jaws had shifted to the arm itself.

It looked as though Urga too would be dragged over the fence, for at first the man forgot that if he let go of her, he could grab for the fencing. But as Bronza and I tried to fight our own captors to let us forward, Urga was allowed to slip to the ground. As soon as the man was fastened in the alligator's jaws, its mates and fellows reared forwards snorting and snarling to share the prize, and still shrieking the man was very rapidly torn apart. Bits of him lurched on

65

the disturbed waters, but soon even those were snapped up. Only the blood remained, a dark suffuse stain. Gradually the creatures quietened, floated off like logs with half-slit eyes, to digest their meal.

We had all stepped back involuntarily to avoid the splatter of blood as the reptiles fought over him. Only the woman had stayed still. There was now a blood-bead, here and there, on her gold gauze. The men cowered.

'The seventh of you is now with the tunnel-demons.'

We had to strain our ears till they almost ached in order to catch her low rustle of a voice.

'There are now three maidens. And three men to capture them. We shall have to see some sport, as my animals have been appeased and yet there can in these corridors be no capture save it be for my animals.

'The maidens will walk on till they come to the place where the water and the fences each side of the path end, and there on the wall hangs a bell, which when they reach it the maidens shall sound, striking it with the rod chained beside it. Then shall I let the men follow them, to do, with them as they will, and for whom they will – priest, prince, queen.'

'But – ' Gurul uttered in consternation. 'The girls simply won't sound the bell – they'll walk past it – we'll lose them – '

'We may then see less sport than we thought,' the woman sighed.

'We have cast long nets to snare these bitches and we can't lose them now – ' Gurul began to bluster.

'My animals are sated, but still obedient – ' the woman said, speaking sharply for the first time, and at her tone the alligators began to look less like logs after all.

The men stepped back again, so far back that in retreating from one fence they banged into the fence on the other side.

'You are rousing my animals,' the woman spoke in a silk rustle.

The torchlight shimmered off her gilded nails as she waved one hand to order us on our way.

We wanted first to fall down at her feet and thank her. We were terrified of omitting any sign of our gratitude, and yet terrified of showing it. She was not predictable. She might be irritated by our delay in simply obeying her, and might change her mind about giving us a start. She might become suspicious – perhaps because she was really putting us on our honour to ring her bell when we reached it.

Giving her speaking glances – though it was hard for us to meet her golden gaze through the gauze and brilliance – we started off, walking as fast as we could without actually scurrying.

At the bend in the tunnel, we left behind us our sight of the three men and the whatever-she-was, and we broke into a run, a dash, in case with macabre humour she now set them after us. So we passed the opening through which she'd come, and it seemed to us only a streak of green light casting a faint phosphorescence for a few yards yet on the tiled tunnel and the alligators and the water and the fencing.

We reached and passed the last of the water. We passed the glint of the chained bell before we realised it. Now we heard a terrible thunder of hooves. The sound seemed to beat all about us, from below and above us, behind, before us, and to every side, even at angles where there was no passage for them to come at us.

'She's put them on horses to catch us,' we panted, for in our trapped panic nothing seemed ridiculous.

But the tunnel narrowed. The ceiling drew down. And ahead was a green growing flicker which presently resolved itself as storm-light into which we had only to step. And leave behind us all those death-trap mazes now only one crumbled stone opening overgrown by moss.

'The hoof-thuds are fading off.'

'She would know horsemen couldn't enter this pipe of tunnel. She didn't send anyone after us.'

'And we didn't even ask her where to find Miyak! Shall we – go back?'

'She meant us for herself, not for horsemen,' Bronza's voice was a new constriction in the narrowed tunnel.

67

'Ahead. Look.' And there we could see the big trees and the swamp orchids. And yet we couldn't quite see them. A film wavered between our eyes and the jungle. I brushed at my eyes. I thought the long dark had blurred them. But the film existed in the tunnel, not in my private vision. It warped in on itself. It seemed to hang like a gaseously transparent veil across the tunnel-mouth a step from us, and to be independently in motion, concentrating itself waveringly into a suction towards us. Even when we saw it for what it was, the children did not run. They waited as insects hang in a web.

There was a malevolence about the thing which turned one's bones to water, as they do turn when one is confronted by an entity unnatural to the rational world of everyday organic decencies and evils. This was sheer grasping alien malevolence, set there to *grab*.

And in spite of the malevolence and the paralysis it put on us, or *because* of it, I was sparked to hope and thence to action. The thing was no accidental phenomenon. It meant evil, therefore it could be countered.

I gathered my will, shook off the miasma – and the very act of doing this, finding you *can* do it in the face of dread from the pit is power-giving – and I took the two steps we'd thought were towards safety, towards the thing.

I heard the children's strangled attempts at warning behind me. I saw and sensed the thing gather itself inwards to wallow and engulf me. I raised my hand, and found my hand had fallen into the old sign that curls the fingers in over the power in the palm, and directs it through two stabbing fingers only. I spoke the word I had learnt from Ooldra in my adolescence.

It was the word Ooldra had used when I appeared in her tent, when she thought me come back from the dead after she had moved to make my death. It was a common or garden mantra, I suppose, nothing most mages don't know. But it was because it was. It hurt, it wounded the thing. The envelope shrivelled and tattered in the tunnel mouth. I ran and the air gave. I was out in the lush swamp. I called to the children, though my tongue felt too swollen to use after the speaking of the mantra, and with incredulous eyes they dashed through the veil as it grew again and yet was not strong enough to grasp them.

'It can't follow us out here,' Bronza wheezed.

'No. But *she* will come to find us caught in it. And she may send anything to look for us once she finds us gone.'

The storm had still not broken. The great drops fell inches apart. Soft shimmer of wind on star-whitened long grass, wild water-flowers and huge crickets, wild keen *oxygen*, my lungs convalescing.

'How did you do it?' they asked me.

'I knew a word –' I said, which already was evident.

We were near tents, which now we discovered between the trees. Low-pitched black tents, and guarded embers, and tethered beasts, some outpost watching the Western marches.

'Hurry past,' Urga whispered. We stooped on into the trees.

'Through the swamp-border, and we'll come out by the ravine.'

'The witch?' I said as we made our way like shadows. 'Who – what is she? Surely, part of the Temple as she is, she should be on the High Priest's side?'

'She's no part of the Temple,' Bronza breathed. 'We were underneath the Temple. Her brutes, and probably she too, have been there long ages and for their own ancient reasons woven in with the roots of religion.'

'Why doesn't the High Priest rid the tunnels of her?' I asked.

'He dare not.'

'You said she's been there ages,' I said. 'Do you – do you mean that she is one of the Changeless?'

Again I felt Urga's brief nod. A tiny thin shiver scampered up my arms. My own witch-nurse, the silver-eyed Ooldra who was my first love and who part-died and then was destroyed in her design to kill me, she who bore my brother Smahil to my father the High Priest and branded him with her sign and put him out to some noble's wife for foster-mother, hoping he would carry her malice through the world – she was one of the Changeless Kind.

*

We were so alert for pursuit that when we saw the black hoods, we knew at once they were *not* looking for us. The radar of our fear would at once have warned us. These were priests hurrying and furtive, sure enough, but on an errand of their own.

After a password sentry-exchanged, hardly distinguishable from the wide pocking of the rain dropping through the excited leaves, the hoods bent and passed into one of the low tents.

'I hate to see your squalid priesthood on good terms with the returned Army,' I said into the restlessness before the storm.

'These are the Northern regiments under the fair turncoat Major who Urga thinks so beautiful,' Bronza said with a sideways look at her sister who remained quiet. 'They may officially be here for our protection – but they're just waiting one word from their King, to turn on us, wrest us from the Dictatress. And who will they get to help them, to spy out the secrets of the Palace for them, and perhaps even assassinate her so that her Army's morale shoots right into its boots? They'll enlist the spies and the hatred of the High Priest.'

'Does she know?' I asked, feeling I should rush to warn the Palace right away.

'Oh, she knows. Wily old cat. She knows everything,' Bronza chuckled, proud. 'She's always one jump ahead of the lot of them.'

'I'd be part of a puma's digestion now if it hadn't been for the fair gentleman you call the turncoat Major,' Urga said austerely.

'You weren't in a position to notice, but close to he looks like a blond snake,' Bronza said in a cheated voice. 'And the talkative Prince is what I really call hideous.'

'He's Prince of What?' I asked.

'Prince Progdin, heir presumptive of our land because

he happens to be a "nephew", well a sort of third cousin actually, of our Dictatress. But more importantly, he's the youngest son of the Northern King over the mountains.'

'The Dictatress has no other heir, then?' I asked.

'A daughter, she had.' Urga flicked a speck of rainbow off her arm, and as it shot away it tendrilled out two tiny legs, and showed itself a speck-size toad. 'But about her the prophecies were very ill.'

'So she was set in a high Tower. She was predisposed to evil, the bones in her body and the blood in her veins were that way. She wanted to fulfil the ill prophecies, bring malice to the land. So she started climbing out of the Tower as soon as she was able to walk. It took her all her childhood to climb down. She made friends with the ravens and jackdaws. She climbed through slits and windows into tiny bad rooms. She tried odd magics. She imitated the rookeries among the turrets and chimneys. She built herself a big nest and lived some years in that. But all the time she was thinking of the ground. When she reached the ground, her breasts had grown and she met the General from the North, the dragon-General whose army eats the flesh of children. She went off with the General, off to the East.' Bronza almost chanted.

'To help him rape the sacred continent of Atlan,' I finished.

'You've seen Atlan, haven't you, Cija?' Bronza said. 'Have you ever seen the dragon-General?'

'I've seen the dragon-General.'

'Is he really plated like a crocodile?'

'No, he is scaled, more like a python. The scales are fine and supple. At first you don't notice them at all. He has quite sensitive skin – they say,' I carefully said.

'Is he really blue?'

'He is the colour of a thundercloud. That's because though his father was human, the Northern King's fiercest General, his mother was one of the big sub-human blue-black females.'

'What is he like?'

'His hair is black and strong, like a mane. He has

71

shoulders, very wide, you know, but he's lean like a dangerous beast. He has black eyes – '

'Has he white to his eyes?'

'Oh, yes,' I said, 'he's quite normal,' and we laughed and around us we heard the trees moaning.

'Our Dictatress hates him,' Bronza said into the wind. 'He and his father before him devastated our land. You can still see the gibbets and the ruins and the cripples. But she is loyal to him. Now that he is Emperor, even over his former master the Northern King, our Dictatress reckons his might is her only protection. After all, she is his regent here. She doesn't want the High Priest to take over.'

'Is there a probability he might?'

'It's all he lives for, plots for, plans for. He is her bitterest enemy. He tries to raise factions of the people against her. He would have her assassinated if he dared.'

'But now *her* Army's back.'

'Yes – but with Northern battalions, under that nasty Major. And Prince Progdin, what's he here for? Not just for intimate spearing-parties in the jungle. His father, the Northern King, is obviously planning his own take-over.'

Hairy orchids trembled with greed as they touched us, as we passed, but when their petals tried to close they found we were not prey after all. Were the disturbances of light natural? Was something about to materialise, barring our way? How was the boy Miyak feeling, lost in the stone dungeons not even knowing whether storm howled or starlight lilted outside? Were they interrogating him about the ex-whore in his mother's household?

'The Northern King wants to overthrow the self-styled Emperor, the dragon-General,' Bronza translated these difficult politics for me. Miyak's fate seemed fatalistically to have been shrugged temporarily aside by the little sisters, as impossible to do any more about, at least for a while. 'You've been over in Atlan, Cija.' (They don't like their brother anyway, I thought.) 'You told us your husband is fighting for the Northern King's daughter Princess Sedili, and her armies, against the Dragon. Soon the Dragon will be overthrown – his army is small and weary, and everyone

72

knows the Atlanteans have no proper army to help him, that the Dragon won Atlan's throne by a trick and not by warfare.'

'When he is no longer undisputed Emperor, the Northern King will hasten his downfall by taking over all *our* country.'

'Or trying. Against our Dictatress, there's already the Temple. And the Major who stopped Urga getting chewed up today.'

'The High Priest,' I mused, 'must be pretty powerful. Cunning, and – and powerful, I mean, your brother just taken off like that, and all those people we saw, even you were in a religious fervour – '

'He's to be reckoned with,' the primrose sister said bitterly. 'I doubt if we'll see Miyak again till we've lost hope. And the man himself works odd horrible little miracles. If he curses anyone,' Bronza added in a low voice, 'they stay cursed.'

Five very large dull-red birds, the colour of sunset on a dying planet, streaked overhead with shricks that would have torn out any human throat attempting them. Their long thin legs caught the drenched foliage and soaked us warmly.

'He put the evil princess in the Tower,' Bronza's little voice continued. 'He wanted to kill her. But the Dictatress was her mother and stopped it. If only he had killed her, she would never have escaped.'

'Was it so bad that she escaped?' I mumbled.

'There were prophecies about her birth,' the child reminded darkly.

'Have you seen the Tower?' I asked.

'It still stands. Like a cadaver, high and still and empty, it watches the ancient deserted bay. We'll show you.'

Behind the birds came the wind. It picked up quite large weights, including curled-up lizards, and hurled them against us.

'Nothing so tenuous as a veil-of-succubus could materialise in this,' Bronza said. 'We are safe here. Except from lightning. Across the fern-gully. Jump.'

Staggering, tottering, we crossed two rolling hills, and fought a red sticky riverlet rushing towards us full of clay down a canyon cut in red rock, and we came to a wide curve of bay. It was a curve that had stayed long years in my inner eye.

Against the sky, jungle pushing behind it, the tall high jut of the Tower.

A surge of something, some intense feeling, I didn't know what, burst inside my breast. That hot secret Tower, with the scorpions and the fountains and the tame turtle and my nurses, always in the back of my memory, the Tower that made me all I am or ever will be, here it was. Not behind my eyes but there before them stretching into the purple panting air.

I'd never been down beside the bay like this.

Nearer than the horizon, chunnels and funnels of sea were being whipped up by the wind. They twisted like vast feeble-minded devil-dancers. In the middle distance, as the waves galumphed at us, the winds seized the foam on their summits and whirled it into cones. Higher and higher rose the waves, like islands, like walls blocking off a half of the sky. Tinier than insects, we watched, crushed by the sight, by the roaring, by the crashing of the explosion as each wave poured down on the reef, creating a wind that nearly catapulted us into the maelstrom.

'Are they tidal-waves?' I asked under the roar. I wasn't quite sure what tidal-waves were, but I knew that if one of these things crashed too far shore-wards, we'd be pulped under water.

'Home is too far. We'll climb the Tower,' Bronza said.

'In this wind?' Urga demurred.

'Better than being caught in waves – or storm.'

'Aren't you afraid?'

'At least there'll be a roof over our heads for the storm tonight. And if we're out all night, Mother may be a little puzzled, more inclined to forgive us tomorrow when she finds that Miyak has been arrested and not us.'

'And do you realise, soldiers may go to Mother's tonight and inquire for us, Temple soldiers.'

'We can get into the Tower through that old pavilion beside it. It used to be the Dictatress' Summer pavilion, but she's abandoned it to be nearer the City unrests. She needs to be in the City all the time now, with things happening so.'

Over the rutty ground we approached the Tower. It grew bigger. It welcomed me in to its aura.

'Don't you feel it's a happy place?' I whispered.

They looked at me. 'The princess climbed out of it,' they said. 'She couldn't bear it. It wasn't evil enough for her to stay in.'

The Tower leaned right over us.

We began to slide up the hill all mottled with lichen, rusty moss. We entered the blue-white colonnades of the deserted pavilion. The stone clanged like metal at our footsteps, the colonnades were so damned empty.

Up staircases veined like cold bosoms, marble as death is. Spiderwebs stretched from step to cornice.

The girls looked brightly about.

'This was all lovely once,' they guessed. They played a game, Let's-pretend-we're-Queens-and-have-come-to-take-over.

'No expense spared?' stipulated Urga.

'No expense spared,' agreed Bronza.

'Right. Well, I'll have a huge cloth of gold curtain there – '

'And I'll stick an urn cut out of diamond here on this parapet to flash the light of the sunrise to the City – '

It was in my mind that here in these dim places, remote from the thunder of the beach, a materialisation would have no difficulties. At times I thought I heard the patter of feet behind us on the marble. Later, in the new hush under the distant reverberations, I could have sworn, though I strained my ears to prove myself wrong, there was breathing in the dark which was not mine and did not fit with the sisters' chatter. Then a blue lightning lit the colonnade and it stretched with all the appearance of long-accustomed emptiness.

We came into places high above the hill.

Still above us stretched the Tower.

'We get on to it by this balustrade,' they said. 'Jump.'

Stones had been placed on the balustrade since my day.

'But the stone is cracked – '

'It's fairly safe, honestly it is.' Effortless the awkward angles of their ankles and knees, grooved with careless little scars like veins of crystallised ginger, already foreshortened above me, angling into their blowing tunics. Their buttocks are so boy-narrow, I don't know how their little modesty-pouches stay up. 'Come on, jump, Cija.'

My knees melted. What about coming back? If we jumped now, we'd have to jump a second time later on – but still my Tower called me. Oh, I wanted to be back in the taut tender intense tight courtyard I was a child in.

I jumped. My hands slid on the rough rock. But my knees gripped, trembling.

*

Hunger attacked us in the dusty courtyard. The storm had still not broken, and the wide drops merely pock-marked the cold old dust. Yearning thirst happened to us in the little gallery with the dry fountain.

Everything seemed smaller. The curtains still hung, white with webs. The powder of desolation lay over everything.

'I think the princess was happy here,' I said.

'There is a library,' they said. 'Would you like to see it?'

My books, which taught me all my misconceptions of the big wide world, were nearly dust. The pages stuck together.

'Here is an old room with a bed full of flies,' they said. 'Such a nice little thin tiled passage twists out of it. Come along it. You can see the mountains across the bay from its other end.'

I stooped and picked something up.

'A shard of ivory . . . There's something painted on it.' They peered over my shoulder. 'Hold it still, Cija.' My hand was shaking. 'Hold it out to catch the next flash of lightning. It's a portrait – a child – do you suppose it's *her*?

76

Throw it away, Cija. Hold your hand, that held it, up in the fresh wind to blow the evil off.'

A portrait, by one of my old nurses, of a child with a high serious forehead, a frown, an eternally rebellious underlip, and grey narrowed eyes staring rebellious to eternity – or, at least, the eternity of a little piece of ivory.

\*

'Look,' I said. 'There's been a fire against this wall, here.'

'Ashes,' they said.

'But ashes soon blow away,' I said. 'Even where it's sheltered, unless it was very recent. This fire was recent.'

'Let's go home. Let's climb down and get home,' Urga said.

'But – ' I said. 'We've a roof here. And after our journey, there may be Temple men waiting.'

'It wasn't children lit that fire,' Bronza said, 'I tell you that.'

We came to the parapet of the Tower.

'Don't climb over,' warned Urga. 'Keep down. Keep your heads down. Now look over there.'

It remained dark. Bronza and I waited for the next lightning.

A small dark cloud detached itself from the jungle west of us and moved rapidly over the hill towards us. The cloud was on the ground, but travelled fast as in an easier element.

'A tribe of them,' Urga said.

'Of what?' I begged.

'I didn't know they'd begun to use this as a headquarters,' Bronza moaned. 'Those droppings we saw – I should have known – I thought they were just from the possums and small apes in the rafters of the palace down there, that sometimes visit up here – '

'Is the tribe heading here?' I asked.

'Gods,' Urga dry-sobbed.

\*

We daren't climb down. The tribe were between us and the hills that meant the City beyond.

Presently, as the wind veered, I could hear the noises from below. The screams and squawks and guttural mouthings, like the continuous gurgling fighting of those rodents called 'devils' because there's no other fit name. And soon we could see the kind of the tribe.

Running on bent legs but so much swifter than apes, their flat heads groundwards, still they looked alert and dangerous. Their arms hung long and muscular. They were covered in matted hair, and the females with clinging young as well.

Urga, Bronza and I gathered the sharpest stones we could find.

We were so panicky that we could be calm only. We had never faced anything like this. This was the approach of the unrational, less rational even than the malevolent unsubstance of the non-thing in the Temple tunnel which anyway had been set there for a reason. Here approached through the thunder something bestial yet more inclined to torture than any true beasts, the approach of a corporate instinct to tear us limb from limb, burgling and rending and savouring and perhaps excited other ways all at the same time. Curiosity itself might incite the tribe to investigate our innards, their elemental intelligence more our downfall than if they were indeed jungle apes.

We had not much time to expect our fate. The creatures bounded up the sides like great primeval squirrels. No sooner had they touched the sides of the Tower than they sprang like balls of rubber setting the force of gravity in reverse.

Pretty soon the first heads appeared level with our own.

Tiny amber eyes, flat and hard as amber, and deep-set under the shaggy brows, stared into ours. With hoarse howls the ape-people leaped over the palisade and advanced upon us.

\*

But they stopped steps from us. They didn't attack at once.

78

They were wary, as of any new thing that they outnumbered and had no need to hurry with. They stopped in a ragged line, even the infants hanging to their mothers' dugs and bellies and backs stopping their wailing and grunting. Eyes and eyes rested on us, flatly summing us up, flatly storing our image into deep mental recesses.

Petrified as the stones in our hands, we stood.

One huge male, seven feet high with his knees bent, opened his mouth in a snarl. The glowering lowering-light hit off his fangs. He let out a roar, a deep roar, thrumming and gathering reverberations like thunder on the prowl round the open courtyard, and started beating on his hard hollow drum of chest.

Bronza could grip her stone no second longer. She drew back her arm. Her stone hit among his busy fists on his chest.

With a bellow he staggered stupidly, taken by surprise. His head swung from side to side, as if searching unbelieving for his attacker.

Now Bronza stood without a stone, and feared trouble worse than if she'd stayed still.

I clutched my sharp rock, hefting it to get it right to thrust with and yet not let go of. I looked for a likely target (victim?).

Even under all that shaggish hair, matted here and there with excreta, brambles and burrs, you could not help noticing that the bulls were excited by the prospect of violence, unless they always carried on like that. I expected sadism therefore. I determined I would kill or maim at least one man-ape, and die fighting rather than in some elemental orgy.

I noted the bull nearest to me, crimson hair quivering over the bulging muscles, his arms hanging forward ready to grab to break, his knuckles almost scraping the old pavings.

I'll twist my stone about in your red gaze, Ape, I thought. I'll blind you while you lunge at me or one of these little sisters.

The leader's roar climaxed in a shriek. He pitched forward on his face.

An arrow stuck deep in his great back.

'What a smashing shot,' breathed Urga beside me, for the huge bull was already dead, his heart neatly split.

The other brutes arrested their charge. They gazed about, menacing but flummoxed. They kept turning and facing different directions.

Up over the side of the parapet appeared several hunters. But these men in shining uniforms were not the Hunters of the Greens. They leaped competently down into the courtyard. The brutes drew aside, as if commanded. They mouthed and throated what were obviously horrible threats. The men ignored them.

'Let's bag a couple more,' one of the men said.

'Isn't one seven-footer enough to carry?' another said. They began at once to start lifting it, and then let out exclamations as they noticed us.

'Hey, the things have been out shopping for dainties!'

'Don't leave us,' Bronza begged in a little toneless wail, after frantically licking her lips at first too dry to get a word out.

Three of the men strode over, and now that they were no longer against the sunk light we could see that one of them was the foreign Prince.

'Holy Heart,' he said, 'the little heroines of the Procession. Don't you get around, children? You owe us an extra debt, I'd say – on top of the price of a mascot puma.'

I didn't like this talk of debts when anyone could see we'd just been in the most mortal terror. Now the ape-people were getting restive. They were working themselves up, and showed plenty of signs of being about to charge in the mass. I kept waiting for the black Prince's signal to leave, but the hunters seemed to delight in striding about in their high tasselled boots amongst the towering shaggy menace.

The Prince stood calmly waiting while soldiers trussed up the slaughtered male, slinging it to a pole for easy carrying. And, most unwisely in my opinion, gutted it too and cut off its head. Apparently such a capture was too commonplace to be worth carrying spectacular in its grotesque completeness through the home barracks. They just wanted it light and compact. But the hacking and the stream of the blood of their fellow so recently alive made the tribe most restive.

'They need quieting down,' the Prince said over his shoulder. 'Kill another, show them who's in control before they attack.'

Over by the far parapet, a spear flashed out of the group of dark soldiers. A female sagged to the stone. But Urga and Bronza started forward appalled at the simultaneous cry of the murdered female – and the wail, very bleak, of her infant.

'It was a mother.' Urga could hardly believe they'd chosen so.

One of the figures, a man who'd been sitting astride the wall, now swung down like a trapeze flier, and ran forward with knife drawn. He pulled the bleeding moaning female, with its tiny one clinging desperately to it, in to the wall by a hand-over-hand grab of his long protruding spear. The wound ripped and the dying blood trickled through the dust and rain. The little apeling, all eyes, uttered pained and bewildered mews.

The man held his knife-hand ready to draw across the baby's throat.

Urga, shouting something incoherent, ran forward and knocked his wrist. The knife went spinning.

'What – ' the man shouted a curse the heavy air shuddered off from. He turned on the girl, snarling, his pale hair raised away under the light helm. 'How am I to get my knife now?'

He stopped. Among the great bulks he regarded the silver girl, all heaving bosom. Recognition came into her angry eyes. He was the man she had so admired, the rider who had saved her from the puma in the Procession. My brother.

'Why did you do that?' he asked in a kinder tone.

'It's only just lost its mother. Don't puzzle it further,' Urga said.

'I was only going to kill it.'

'That was puzzling it. It's not hurt. But look at its poor eyes.'

The figure who paced up behind interposed. This figure was the black-a-vised Prince from the North.

'What would you do with it, girl?' he asked severely in a dark colourless tone. 'Leave it to die in the swamp, starving and orphaned, for your sentimental whim, till its kindred set on it to rend it apart?'

'We could feed it,' Urga said.

Without seeming to attend to her, Smahil took a dagger from his belt. He sliced open the infant's neck. Blood covered his hand and the hilt. The tribe shuffled, appalled, cowed. Urga sprang nearer with a cry as though he'd wounded her.

'You killed it after all I said!' Urga accused wildly.

'It would have died unless expertly tended,' Smahil carelessly said. 'And do you suppose your good mother would have let it in her home?'

Bronza let out a crack of laughter. 'You know her?'

'I have not that pleasure,' Smahil bowed.

I drew back into the gloom. I pulled the shadows around me. I watched his glance run up and down and up the two sisters, particularly white Urga who must seem to him vivid with the passion of her pity. She stared on him, her own gaze violet with the reaction of her daring to be angry with him. She was in doubt. She found him unlikeable now that she breathed face to face with the stranger-rescuer of the Procession.

The men trussing the three apes shouldered them up on their poles.

'Smahil,' the Prince jerked his heavy head.

Smahil bowed to Bronza. And hesitated insolently, a smile flickering over his narrow lips, before omitting the bow to Urga.

'Only one of you need walk,' he said. 'Up with you, righteous. You'll direct your road to me.'

82

Smahil took possession of his spear with his narrow hands, one white, one red.

He held one to Urga. It was the red hand. She hesitated, then put her own into it.

Smahil stood to the wall, and straddled it. He swung Urga up before him, cradling her, and then she was tossed over his shoulder.

We were all of us over the parapet. So swiftly I had no time for terror, we were down, across the cracked balustrade and in the empty palace.

By the time Bronza and I were on the ground, we had time just to see Urga mounted before Smahil on a big Northern bird. Urga's hair flowed across Smahil's arm, and his mount set off at a swift unsmooth gallop in a bright direction.

'Cija!' Bronza called. 'Are you down? She's gone, our little sister, with the fancy lord. Cija!'

Smahil's head snapped back as though pulled by cord. The pale blaze of his eyes stabbed into my heart. But it was a questing gaze. He couldn't see, and doubted if he'd heard. Already far off among the rocks, carried at a fast uneven jog by his ugly mount, he disappeared with Urga beneath the great glooms on which the storm brooded.

'How did you get up with that crew up there?' the men with us asked in the liveliest wonder (and now the tribe were leaning down bombarding us with old stones which fell from such a height with quite a velocity).

Bronza and I explained, though it was difficult to talk with our hearts going so hard. The men told us to praise our Gods (congratulating themselves) that they'd been stalking the tribe today and happened to come along as they did. The Prince said no more at all, except finally, 'Bring them with us to the City Palace.'

'To the Palace?' I stammered. 'Oh, no, no –'

'Don't be crazy, Cija,' Bronza said. 'It's too late and far now for us to be spared an escort home, but we're being offered a night in the *Palace* gosh instead of being set down to find our own way.'

'Father, Mother, they'll worry – ' I said, desperately.

Bronza turned eyes of amazement on me.

'Prince Progdin,' I said, suffering an eerie sensation addressing my mother's heir, the man destined to sit the throne mine by birth, 'I must get back to my child . . . '

He spurred his mount and my plea dangled amongst hurried hooves.

*

So we clattered into the Palace courtyard as the torches were sconced.

Still, still the storm had not broken. By now a deathly stillness lay behind every sound. The torch-flares took it in turns to cower as though beaten oppressed by the weight of the atmosphere, or to stream out like naphtha.

'Sorry we couldn't take you to your Mum's,' said one of the Prince's bodyguard (who had, in fact, done exactly that) as he helped me down from the thoroughbred he'd shared with me. 'But it's our supper now, you see; and after that, for those of us not on duty on guard, time's our own – and none of us is going off on someone else's errands when he can be off on his own.'

'Where do we eat?' asked Bronza, all ready for the next stage.

'With us, I suppose, because I'm asterisking sure it's not with the Prince,' one of the guard guffawed.

'Is he monkish?' Bronza asked, helped down.

'Eh?'

'Your Prince. He's all celibate and so on, isn't he?'

'He'll be a bloody good Dictator,' said the guard.

*

I liked the bathroom better than the supper. It was a fair supper, good strong stew and lots of barracks-meat.

But the conversation was that dreadful infantile kindergarten sort you get from men in a little world of their own – all heartily thrilled and proud that it sounds a closed shop to outsiders, all little catchwords and rogueish asides and secret winks and Well of course knowing old *Shorty* – and aren't the outsiders glad it's a closed shop. Even the little

84

sister, ready to drink in open-mouthed the glamour of the royal private guard, was soon bored to tears and couldn't eat properly she yawned so often.

'I wonder what – if – Miyak's eating?' I said, worried not to see her more worried.

'Ah, I don't doubt he's still all in one piece,' she said. 'I'm wondering what Urga's having now. Do you suppose the flashy Major has suggested some wine while the rain holds off?'

A misery stirred in my heart and groin and I tried to concentrate on the table-talk.

There was also an awful lot about girls (waggishly referred to as the fair sex). To listen, you'd think no female could so much as pass one of these oafs on the other side of the street without an unfightable urge to rush over all lubricous. Perhaps they were waiting for us to suffer the Urge. They paid so little attention to us they wouldn't even pass us the salt, made us reach for it.

I'm no raving beauty. But what about the delicious adolescent with me? Were all these super-virile dashingly wicked boasters really wet dish-rags? Well, of course, us being the Prince's guests-by-order, there wasn't much hope of starting anything with us.

Bronza, disappointed, started a game with herself.

She made rather lopsided towers in her stew and sent little ape-beans and lentils skidding down the sides. This too was kindergarten stuff but she had no shame. I looked up at the geckoes relaxing happily upside down on the stone ceiling.

Somewhere up there, too, separated from me by a mere mile or so of gallery and colonnade and maybe a few banqueting chambers and halls of state, my mother the Dictatress was picking at her supper or beating a slave or wondering whether she'd ever again see her vagrant daughter Cija who could be so useful in any number of entrancing new plots.

Our meal ended abruptly and the soldiers all sprang up and stiffly saluted my mother's flag.

Outside the arrow-slits high in the walls, the green post-sunset pre-storm lay almost limpid. I could imagine the stone silvered green on the great causeway spanning the Royal Canal in which the foundations of the Palace stand gently rotting century after century.

'Now, ladies – ' said a pudgy captain with a bristly neck and soup-stains on his uniform.

'May I request a bath?' Bronza the Prince's guest superbly said.

She was thinking of the tepid wash-water at home, even without the orange scum over it because Miyak had already shaved in it. I stood beside her.

An impatient corporal was detailed to show us to the officers' bathroom. He was to wait till we were finished, then lead us to our whitewashed dormitory peaked under the eaves. With Bronza still luxuriously splashing in there, he got desperate at the prospect of having to wait as long for me again.

He sidled up against me and spoke intimately in my ear.

'If you're quiet and quick, miss,' he said, 'can I trust you? Can I take you along to one of the bathrooms for the Royal family's guests? It's adjoined to the suite reserved for the Prince's friend, the Northern Major, and he's not in residence at this time. So if you was quick, and quiet – '

'You'd be off duty sooner,' I agreed. 'Fine by me.'

*

The bath reserved for my Smahil is all pristine white tiles – except for the bottom. This is glass, through which you can see down into the huge lavish aquarium stocked with wavy weeds, clouds and bubbles of microcosmic live exotica, and a ghastly conger. In spite of the big soft towels, and the gentle rainbows beaming through the window of glass stained vividly, I didn't bask long. Not for pity of the guard, but because it's an acquired taste, to relax in the illusion that you're sharing your bath with a conger.

Smahil does, however, apparently go in for mixed bathing. There are scents (crushed from rather sickly flowers) standing about in curlicued bottles with bows round their

86

necks and bells tinkling off their stoppers. And in a cup-board badly latched beside the rather austere un-curtained bed glimpsed through the latticed door, there was a bunch of silky this and thats like pastel vapour.

As the conger pursued me out of the spice-smelling water, and into a thirsty towel, I noticed the pale glint of a single short hair spiralled across one of the tiles. It had a split end. Smahil's hair shouldn't have split ends, I auto-matically thought. Is he undernourished, or not getting enough deep sleep?

*

Hurrying with the soldier, back along the gracious corri-dors, back to the guard-quarters. A group of girls were billowing towards us in their pretty gowns and ruffles over full pretty pastel trousers. To prove they were ladies, and never walked more than a few steps, they had bare feet with rouged insteps, and their pert breasts were rouged too under their filmy ruffles.

I thought they'd just flutter past, they looked like ladies-in-waiting because of having been born to minor nobles, that sort of rosy-cheeked bright-ringleted pudgy-chinned little lady.

But one of them stopped in mid-giggle.

Fresh-faced little dear, I thought. I was only sour. I wouldn't much mind rosy cheeks, nor bright ringlets. Nor enough nice nosh to fatten up my face.

She said to my soldier, 'When do you expect to see him next?' She asked in a voice of mystery, but so the others could all hear if they strained their ears. Which they did.

'Likely tomorrow,' the soldier's voice, too, was very conspirator.

'Then give him this.' She fished about in her bodice and produced all warm, crumpled and slightly moist a letter. From her itty purse of metal beads she conjured a coin. She pressed both into the soldier's palm. She glanced at the other girls all agog, and said in a slightly lower tone, but quite unnecessarily, 'Tell him it's about our next Assig-nation.'

87

The fountains beside us breezed about as an old lady panted down the corridor.

'My sweet lady Katisa, no gossiping with the military – what if you were seen – what would the Palace think – ah, you are all so tricksy – have to keep my poor old eyes on you the entire time – ' The ladies burst into fits of the giggles at her and the old chaperone went on scolding them till the soldier, with me, had nearly sidled past. Then the chaperone turned on him. 'No canoodling with our young ladies!' she wagged a sharp finger. 'You know the rules! You know the well-deserved penalty!'

The soldier folded the note (and coin) tightly out of sight in the sweaty folds of his hand. 'Yes, ma'am, oh, indeed, ma'am.' He was most humble.

But suddenly the old lady was back against the wall. Her hand flattened against her sagging breast. Her eyelids and chin and nose were shaking against each other.

'Are you having an attack, Snedde? Are you all right, dearie?' the young ladies flurried around.

'Oh – my baby – my baby – ' the old lady improbably moaned.

At their calling her Snedde, my recollection flashed. This old quivering stick in a floss of flowery silk and bell-bottom trousers, this was my old nurse Snedde! I'd never liked her, but I longed very much to run to her and hug her and say, 'There, there, I'm your baby and I never forgot you, how excited I am to see you – ' but this was a horribly dangerous situation. I walked on very swiftly. The soldier was quick to follow me. Round the corner, I started to run. 'We're a bit late, aren't we?' I panted to the soldier. 'That's right, you get back there before me,' he muttered. 'For Gods' sakes, don't say where you've been. I'd run too if I was allowed.'

Dear sweet lovely Gods, my mind gibbered, don't let the old half-wit tell those simperers who I am.

*

The dormitory we shared with two pages only, one of whom doused the light and promptly slithered across into

88

the other's bed, where in spite, or because, of the extreme narrowness they were soon so immersed that we had privacy to talk as we liked.

The room was so close, I wasn't aware the tiny window was open – till big black floating flakes began to drift through on to my arm and coverlet. At first I thought of rain, then snow – and starting up from my murmuring bed, saw the glow in the sky.

'Fire,' I said. 'The City is alight,' and even that did not impinge on the squirming squeaking pages.

Bronza and I went to the window.

We could see the glow and the flicker, but no sounds reached up.

'No,' she said. 'The Temple. But the City soon.'

'You know,' I said, 'that we could be blamed for this. It was the torches of our pursuers that set the bedding alight in the children's court.'

'Yes,' she said. 'If they have failed to terrify Miyak (which is most unlikely, I am sure they must already have got his address from him), now they can pin the fire if nothing else on you. The whore-master must be determined to get you back. A very thrifty man. Why don't we just offer to return him the coins he paid for you?'

'I don't like to be here,' I said, thinking uncomfortably that I should no longer stay at 'home' either. 'They can too easily trace us here.'

'But we're the guests of the Prince.'

'The Prince is on the side of the priests.'

'They'll soon have that fire out. They've probably just discovered it. It must have been smouldering unnoticed till it burst out. They'll have it under control already.'

'Let's go, Bronza.'

'They may be waiting for us, the Temple men, when we reach home.'

'I think I'd better not accompany you.'

'Very wise,' she said after hesitating. 'But don't go off on your own. Remember your baby. Scout around and wait for our all-clear.'

'How to get out now?'

'The ways won't be locked in a big Palace.'

I don't think the pages noticed our going.

There were sentries on all the stairs. But we pulled our cloaks over our heads and slipped easily past. There were plenty of other such comings and goings. We weren't in the places where assassination must be feared, and I suppose the sentries hereabouts were on the look-out only for punitive forces, all clank and clangour. If they were on the look-out at all.

Over the causeway, after just a few of the little adventures you can't avoid in a Palace night, the accosts and pawings and little pursuits. The glow already fading. A tattered shape, very big, flapped across the stars. In Atlan it might have been a flying dragon. Here it was probably merely a pterodactyl preying late.

'The rain. It's burst at last.' Bronza held out her hand and the drops gathered in the hollow of it and the stars were drenched. 'That's what has faded the fire.'

'It's become hail!' For as we spoke, the rain solidified, and the alleys were full of clatter and hurrying beggars.

'There are no soldiers about. None. We worried for nothing. Mind these steps, they're slippy.'

At the house I pulled back, though my cloak was black and stinging. '*He'll* be in there with Urga ahead of us!' I wailed. 'Come in, come in,' Bronza dragged me in. But the kitchen was empty.

*

Till midnight, till dawn it came down. Still, no wind. Still no Urga. Just the heavy hail, dropping and dropping till we thought the creeper and all the nests would be washed away.

'It's like being under a descending sea,' I whispered.

'The hedgehogs and such under the house will be swimming now,' Bronza whispered.

Whispers were quite clear, in a kind of reverberant void under the rain-noise, like talking into the faint enclosed waves in a sea-shell even though the tide is coming in around you.

Behind the drawn curtains, we winced from the lightning's spasms.

'Listen to the dogs howling below stairs,' I continued this inventory of animal disturbance.

'Bet she's having a marvellous time somewhere now,' Bronza said. 'She'll have a lot to tell us tomorrow. Listen, there's Father squelching out to his compost heap.'

'To commune with it?' I was fascinated even from my visions of Smahil sheltering Urga under a tree, or Smahil wining Urga in a tavern, or Smahil saying to Urga, 'The barracks is nearer. Come up to my quarters and wait.'

If he'd walked Urga into his bedroom as I bathed with the conger in his bath, with what polished aplomb would he have greeted me?

'He's putting sacking over it. This heavy rain will worry him. It disturbs it. Gods, he waxes passionate over that compost heap. Always adding new gunge to ferment in its own sultry heat. Turning the outer sides with a pitchfork every few weeks so it all gets its fair share rotting.'

'I did wonder why he saves bacon rind like some people collect marbles. And I sort of wondered why he snatches chewed bones from the dogs.'

The creeper tugged and strained. It sounded as if it was being torn by its roots from our walls. Where was Smahil? Why wasn't Urga home?

'We'll break the news about Miyak to Mother tomorrow, when Urga is back.'

'If she ever is.'

The hail struck like stones on the window. The casement rattled. All through the house, hinges strained. Finally, this lulled us off.

We woke in clear soft light.

'It's *sun* light!' Bronza cried, flinging wide the curtains.

She opened the beaded, starred, dazzling window. Sweet air sped into our room.

We opened the door, tugging our tunics over our heads, and Fernak who had slept outside followed us down the stairs, his fur looking like it had just got a good brush. It must have been on end during the lightning.

Father, all blackly hairy under the brief cloak that was all he'd had time to fling on, was belting out to uncover his compost, which apparently relishes mild moist showers as much as it abhors heavy cats and dogs.

And after him with the pitchfork burpled Miyak.

He swaggered at us.

We wouldn't ask, so after waiting in vain he had to tell us anyway. 'You don't know what I've survived. Racks, they showed me. Little pincers and tweezers. They got where I lived out of me, and asked me how many in my family, and their names, and so on. I said Cija is a cousin of ours, which means to disprove that she's a citizen with rights they'll have to search her out in the annals of the Registry and a ghastly task that will be. Even if they can read.'

'They sent "soldiers", Temple ragamuffinry, to sort you out,' Father said from the compost. 'But we satisfied them.'

'But they must have found Seka – they'll be back – '

'They won't be back,' Father said with the greatest finality. Why did I believe him? Why didn't I question him further? Because he seemed willing to take on his own head, and his household's, the risk of harbouring me – and I was too weak to insist on finding another home. 'Not a word to the better half,' he said. 'She doesn't know about any of it.'

'It's a glory-be morning!' the remaining sister cried.

'Nits, it's pouring steady,' said Miyak whose room is the other side of the house.

This house is on a hill. From the topmost window, a junk-filled attic cupboard-size under the eaves, we could see one side of the hill drowning in a grey downpour, the other side a tossing sea of sparkling grass drying under a sunbright breeze straight from the big fresh larynx of Spring.

*

'Mother, Mother, I'm alive, there's no need to worry,' Urga cried as she raced in to breakfast.

92

'I didn't know you weren't in your bed,' Mother grunted. 'What's this gallivanting?'

'I was just now brought home by the ex-patriate Major,' Urga stopped. She knew Mother's puritanical code.

'He took you a long way round then,' Bronza insinuated.

'You didn't bring him in to say hello?' Mother said. 'So I brought you up with alley manners, did I?'

Urga's bloodshot eyes narrowed on Miyak but she tried to concentrate as she confessed, 'He wasn't interested – I did invite him in. But we talked and talked at the barracks while the storm lasted. He smells of sweat and leather. He fed me rum and Northern goat-yoghurt. He asked me what do I think of men, and I said I don't know any. He says I shall know, if I walk by the outpost tonight so he meets me.'

'You might bring home some pretty perks from a friend-ship like that,' Mother omitted any warnings to take care. 'Those soldiers in the Northern camp get all sorts of privileges.'

'You aren't going?' Bronza said. 'You can't stand him.'

'I can stand him.'

'Well, the storm did what the man invoked it to do,' Father said.

It's hard to tell, when you don't know a culture, whether a man is being superstitious, or joking.

'You mean it brought on the Spring, like strong liquor bringing on a woman's month?' Miyak said.

'I mean our Army is cantoned right round the City's three land-slides, and the marshes are no danger.' Father in a rare live mood tossed little Aega gurgling in the air.

*

'Watch those girls,' Mother bodingly said to me, today. 'They have their reasons, I don't doubt, for all this friend-liness to you.'

*

'Cija must have a room of her own,' this Mother said in the blowing Spring. Every soul felt like energy. This Mother

93

felt benevolent as a hostess. They cleared the junk, the old antlers and the bottled blood of ancestors and the sucked out brontosaurus eggs, out of the attic, the smallest highest room. It is just big enough to hold my narrow bed and a big basket with rugs for Seka, and a chest to fold our clothes in. The window is the roof, sloped at by the house's walls running, racing to their highest point.

I lie on the bed and watch the window right above me, just room for me to stand without knocking my head on the clumsy distorting glass, and if I stand I can stand with my face half out, if the window is open, out under the breeze or the rain sluicing down the slanting pane and gathering in a spasm of mirror-bright drops to fall and soak the counterpane, all patchworked by grandmother fingers, worms now.

I like the mauve breeze of twilight best, and the stars burning their brand on my forehead when I go to sleep.

*

Come evening, we perch like storks along the spine of the roof. We dangle our legs. Down either side of us, down slopes the blonde thatch lavishly sprinkled with flowers growing wild amongst the smocked straw. Below, the neighbourhood children, and boys and wenches, are still splashing each other from the endlessly fascinating well. The well-splashes below, and the huge sky breathing around us, grow sweetly steadily different. The day sky is vast. But the innocent blue of a little bird's first egg. The Summer night is light as day, only it's violet light.

'Out prick the pin-point stars,' Bronza by my shoulder softly remarks.

'I wonder how the night was millennia ago when there was a Moon in the sky?'

'I don't believe in that old legend. It's so preposterous that it's against nature. The priests have forgotten their own symbolism.'

'I don't believe it either, but I like to pretend I do. Pulling stronger tides than we can have, a big white light at

94

night. The sun's sister. It must have been hard to commit night-crimes by stealth in those old ages.'

*

A man in a lighted tavern doorway.

It was Smahil. I started back to him as if propelled. My throat had gone dry. I had to suck saliva into my mouth to get ready his name that I wanted to cry and could just whisper.

It wasn't Smahil.

The light on his hair had deceived me, and something about the way he stood. He was taller and heavier. He was browner.

He stepped across the pavement to me.

I could see his wide grin and unclean teeth.

'Well, birdie,' he said.

I turned and ran.

Just a look lingering on a man, and the man is hurrying to accommodate you.

My bed gets emptier every night. Each day the tax-ridden priest-ridden citizens who call or catch at me in the street are uglier.

Of course I wonder sometimes what sort of prostitute I would have made. Useless, I think. I believe you have either to be mad keen all the time no matter what on earth they're like. Or absolutely uncaring, as if your body were nothing to do with you, just a hole in the wall. I live in my body. It's the only stronghold I and Seka have left.

*

'I've been robbed!' I am furious though I tried to sound merely indignant.

'It must have been some child.' They didn't name their little sister Aega who immediately came to my mind. 'No decent burglar would take such silly little things.'

'And leave behind for me some fairly valuable things,' I agreed. My clothes hadn't been touched. But my dragon-fly on a pin, and the wooden boat Ogdrud carved out of a large nut-shell for Seka, have been taken. With such an

95

irrational thief, I suppose it was touch-and-go whether they'd fancy this Diary and the incredibly ancient maps I brought out of Atlan. But those were still safely stowed under my dresses in the chest, though the top layers of clothing had been mussed.

Now I sat turning the maps over. I've hardly looked at them since I left the secret continent. I've found them distasteful. Not just because they were the sorceror's, but because of a peculiar coldness that strikes off them into your fingers as you touch them, a radiance of cold energy that strikes your flesh if you bend close over them.

I kept them because it would have been a crime – or simply impossible – to throw away anything so ancient.

But I can't even make much out of the crissing and crossing of smeary ink-lines, like the trails of a tired old slug among the crackings of the parchment.

Is the homunculus still roaming the woods behind the haunted castle?

(Am I now among the castle's ghosts?)

A terror, is it, to the birds and beasts of the hill? And a growing puzzle to itself as it sees that all living things are born, and have an infancy, saving itself only?

Oh well. After all, a homunculus is not unknown to nature. After all, some 'true' life is spontaneously generated – everyone knows that bundles of old clothes, if left long enough, produce little mice – and that barnacle geese are born from salty old tree stumps.

'Whoever it was,' Urga later said as we kicked our heels on the thatch, 'they got in through the roof-window. Look, do you see those big marsh-mud footsteps dried all over the thatch?'

I woke. I screamed.

Instantly the face withdrew from the window directly over my bed. But I knew, from the swift sounds of getaway over the roof, the slight sway of the rafters and then the rustle in the nearest trees, I hadn't imagined it.

The stars had hung behind the face – but I'd seen the long red fur, the tongue slipping reflective across the fangs, the brow-shadowed gaze of the intent brute.

# PART THREE
# THE PALE VISITOR

URGA doesn't dislike Smahil. Obviously he doesn't dislike her. Has he noticed how much cleaner her navel is these days? He gave her the huge fine smoked ham of intimate bear meat, all glazed and rosy and spiked with cloves, that tided us over the hunters' bad fortnight. He gave her the odd mark like a violet puncture on her neck that she came home to shiveringly show her sister and me. 'It felt he was melting my neck. *Shall I stop?* he said. *Why, are you drawing blood?* I moaned and he laughed and I begged him not to stop! Never knew it would make a mark.'

'Your Major doesn't realise he's dealing with an innocent,' I said severely. 'He must have thought you knew it would leave this mark, but didn't care.'

'I wouldn't have cared,' Urga said simply.

'Now you'll somehow have to hide the mark.'

'Yes, Mother would kill me. But she keeps nagging me to bring him home. Like a trophy for the wall. She wants him to have serious intentions about setting me up somewhere. He's not interested in coming home. He says I'm a bore about it – '

'Better to send him packing before he starts taking – and like all men completely stops giving.'

'You're a withered-up frustrated old spinster, Cija,' Urga pouted. 'Well, honestly, luv, you talk like one, honestly. If that husband of yours doesn't rejoin you soon, you must decide on a lover.'

'One of the local boys?' I said scornfully.

'Anyone,' Urga said with an expansive gesture.

'You are very generous,' I said wryly.

Lover? The word means one man to me. One man, forbidden to me by every law of man and Gods for ever, the lean pale man who put the mark on Urga's neck.

*

Today the High Priest reached out again his arm to kill me.

It was evening. Beyond the City, the mountain peaks floated on the twilight. The dark river swiftened with the sounds of boys in their canoes catapult-killing river-rats as they emerged from their holes in the steep wet banks and were spotted in the prow-flares.

Bronza and I mooched towards the Greens, our arms heavy with boughs of blossom we didn't need at home because the same trees breed like rabbits in Mother's yard.

'I think Urga should be careful of that Major,' Bronza said. 'I don't think he thinks of her as more than a sort of pet.'

I was surprised. I'd been careful to say nothing like this. It is none of my business. Whatever I say, I suspect my reasons.

'Can she look after herself – if she wants to?' I said after a pause. It was the least loaded, most disinterested of the remarks that crowded to my lips that have been hungry, thirsty for this for nearly four years and must *must* stay so till I die.

'She's no match for him,' Bronza irritably kicked a rabbit skull. The woods and banks were full of the cries of little trapped animals, because the woods and banks were also full of steel springs springing to, wooden shutters shutting down, nets suddenly tightening, tiny hearts beating horrendously. Was Urga like one of these little hearts innocently approaching the invisible spread of the fine mesh?

Selfishly, I didn't like to say too much about how she should be warned – in case I felt I was saying it in hope of keeping her away from him.

I know Urga doesn't *want* to be warned.

We weren't alarmed as a pound of feet pounded behind us. But they didn't pass us. Suddenly Bronza and I were knocked against each other. Clinging to each other in automatic reaction, we belatedly discovered we were flung together in some sort of container that gave but would not break as we struggled. In the dark, our captors and our envelope were invisible. 'We're in a magic,' Bronza said. 'No,' I said, 'a great net.' It was so like what I'd just been thinking about Urga, that it might have been a sort of thought transference.

'You sods, let us out!' Bronza's fists tried to beat the net that gave and mocked her.

We were rolled on top of each other as our envelope was pitched into something else bigger and wooden. Branches and twigs thrust at my eyes. I started to yell and found I was biting on the weed-blossom we'd been holding. A little something started spiralling up one of my nostrils – a tiny spiderlet from its cave of petals?

Simultaneously we both rolled over and started to scream 'Helphelphelp!'

'Stow that.' A thrust, the heavy blunt end of a pole or oar, under my rib nearly winded me.

'No helphelp forthcoming,' Bronza said. 'This river is used to cries for help. No one pays attention. Every pair of ears on this river is plugged with indifference.'

There were sploshes. We were rolling. We were in motion. 'We are going somewhere,' I whispered, trying to coax the spider out of my nose.

'We're in a boat,' Bronza guessed. 'We're moving down-river – look, see by the stars.'

And I suddenly asked: 'Hasn't the High Priest a private island five miles down-river?'

'What's that to do with anything?' Bronza asked. 'Some rotten nobles have picked on us for some rotten orgy. We must try to get away. These orgies can be dangerous.'

Out with it, Cija. 'The High Priest is my father.' Before the completion of her gasp and her thought *Is poor Cija round the bend*, I added, 'He wants to kill me.'

'Cija!'

'It's my fault you've been dragged into this. I'll get you out somehow,' I promised, polite and mendacious as any good guest. (Only I suppose now Bronza was my guest.)

'I don't think they mean to kill us,' Bronza said. 'They

99

could have done it, instead of this kidnapping.'

'So, what goes on on the holy island?' I inquired.

The religious Bronza wouldn't answer. 'If you're right,' was all she would grunt, 'we'll find out soon enough.'

*Now*, more than in the labyrinth last month deep under the Temple as Gurul's will to capture us strained unsuccessfully against the alligator witch's own greed for us, *now* I felt my father's malice closing, like the net, like thin endless fingers, around me.

The man (or whatever he is) who spawned me, brought *me* and all I know as *me* and have known as *me* through all my ineffectual terrible adventures, he wills my death, he will bring about my death as he did my existence.

Is there in me anything of him?

Well, I must doubt that, mustn't I? I am sure my father must be logical, analytical, cold as a brilliant stalagmite (or stalactite, as he's supposed to be a visitor from a supernatural plane) – with a keen mind, one of those brains that wind round every possibility before the thing happens.

There was one possibility he didn't forecast.

Our boat ground to at what must be a landing stage.

'Journey's end,' I said very, very grimly.

'Something'll happen,' Bronza said through chattering teeth. 'I know help will happen somehow. Well, I mean, I want to hear your story for a start, holding out on us you've been, girl. Urga will help. She'll know I'm in trouble.'

It was my turn, wasn't it, to be incredulous?

'We're twins, you know,' Bronza whispered into the weeds in the kidnap boat while Urga shyly teased Smahil some miles to our east, 'two sisters of one wombing.'

'But you're not identical twins.'

'We always know when the other's fed up. We have our periods the same week,' Bronza said vaguely.

She wasn't as depressed as I was, as our net was hauled ashore and we stood upright in it. Well, she isn't my father's daughter.

'March, you cows.' We were shoved along by another oar.

'High Priest *celibate*,' Bronza hissed her afterthought as we stumbled onwards.

'My father,' I reiterated, 'set his heart on killing me.'

*

What could we see to either side of our way? Not much, what with dark and net jogging with us. I had to keep my gaze beaded on the jug-eared head of the man in front, otherwise I strayed and stumbled and pulled Bronza stumbling with me, and the guard behind jabbed and cursed.

But I was sure, from the shyness of the stars, that it wasn't just strands of net above me and Bronza. Strands of foliage.

Was I right? Were we on the High Priest's secret island? Or was this the approach to some feast, where we were to be part of an enthusiastic host's entertainment, perhaps horribly pregnant by morning, perhaps mutilated anonymous bodies cast out on the morning river to feed the rats.

Yes, foliage above. Close above. Mooping of sleepy wings flurried by our rough passing. Slither of lizard feet on a bough. Scrape, indignant dog-bark of retreating monkeys. Sudden scamper against the net of small lank reptile started across our path.

Then lights blazing ahead. The meagre torches of our guard paled to insignificance.

Gods, I prayed with a jolt as I nearly slid backwards. This is getting steep.

'Are we on a mountain?' I asked the nearest guard.

He wouldn't answer, then decided it was better to be sadistic and spine-chilling than just maddening and uncommunicative.

'You *might* call it that,' he said in an indescribably sinister voice. 'But the centre of this is a little more – upsetting – than old volcanic fire and brimstone, I can tell you.'

Now the last short climb to the blazing lights more above us than ahead of us. Horribly steep. Still the ankle-tickling ferns, but now they seemed just a tissue, a layer over stone. Stone, very hard and reverberant, underfoot.

101

We came to a halt.

Bronza and I, and I think the guards as well, were breathing heavy. My knees felt a bit watery, as if any minute they might fold.

I resented the fact that Bronza was there, human clutter. I felt my death a private thing, and like all private things should be savoured without the distractions of guilt because of a companion's fate.

A great rumbling and shuddering seemed to come from the ground beneath our feet. My insteps ached. I felt I must grip, almost needing suction to keep my place on this last terrible slope.

The earth grumbled.

'Lower them into the abyss,' said the dark voice of a man who had ridden up. I tried hard to see him, or anything at all, but the net was too thick.

And then, as we in the net were picked up bodily by several grunting straining bodies, and swung forwards amidst a smell of sweat and crushed fern, that dark voice said: 'What's that glint in the net?'

'One girl's a bit deformed, sir. Ever so fair, almost one of them albinos.'

There was a slashing – was it a sound or a flame? I was conscious of something sharp – or was it just very bright? – parting the strands by my face and shoulder. I sprang out and hurled my limp-blossomed boughs in the nearest man's face. But he caught them and just stood, like an awkward suitor with a big bouquet. On a pony that was darkness except for its liquidy eyes and the diamonds studded in its hooves, sat a big broad-shouldered silhouette. It was his sword that had slashed our big portable prison.

'Let's see the flies before we deliver the web,' he said expressionlessly. 'The spider loves to wait.'

(The image struck a chord. Yes, my Father, yes, a spider gleefully waiting, rubbing together in anticipation its six legs, hugging itself with its six arms, open beak slavering at the expectation of the helpless feast.)

The blade reached out and flicked Bronza on the shoulder. She dare not move.

102

'Is this,' the dark voice inquired, 'she?'
'No, lord. The other.'
The silhouette swivelled in my direction.
'The accursed one, the forbidden birth.'
The guards shuffled. It seemed the dark rider voiced a secret rumour, an idea that should remain unspoken, that took on danger as well as life if it were let from men's mouths. This time no one affirmed or denied.
'This one shall go free. Her sin was only to have been caught with the accursed. Loose her.' He pointed at Bronza. 'Kill her' – He pointed at me – 'Down to the Watcher with her.'
They pulled Bronza away from me. I stood alone on the peak of the – what was it? Around and about, I saw the drowning mirror of the great river, and beyond, the sea into which is debouched. Above, and down there too, lay none too brightly the stars. Shapes passed them swiftly. Wind-whipped clouds, yes, flying dragons, yes, the leathern beat of a pteranodon. We stood at the tip of a steep hill, the others apart from me as if I were indeed accursed. They stepped forward to lay hands on me, to fling me down the black crack that yawned before us splitting this artificial mountain   artificial, yes, for though from the distant river or far banks it must seem clothed with forest, a natural retreat, now I saw the paving stones, it was all a great pyramid, tree-grown. Bronza shrieked, 'Leave her! Leave her alone!' but even to her I must seem accursed if I were the thing I claimed to be, the born child of the sacred celibate Highest with his Gods' blood in his ageless veins – the dark Prince Progdin sat his dark pony, waiting impassive. The guards' hands were on me – and then another voice rang out, a new voice, hoarse. One of the guards had been sent spinning, and far down we heard his splash as already a corpse he smashed the water, two more were bent gasping as blood gouted between their fingers on their wounded arms, before I realised what the hoarse sound had been. It had been a word. The word had been my name, 'Cija.'
Regaining my own balance, I teetered on the brink of the chasm. Inviolate gloom stretched down eternally into

it. My head swung limp, Someone sprang forward and seized me away from the edge. I saw the stretch of the pyramid below me. To think we had climbed that! Now that I knew the thin covering of top-soil for what it was, I couldn't believe we had not pulled it off, and all the writhen roots in it, with our clutching feet.

I stared up into a swift savage face. I saw from below a fierce jaw, two dilated nostrils and all at once the face turned down to me and Smahil's eyes, pale even in this dark, blazed down on me.

His heart tom-tommed so it hurt my side against it. I was in a strange grip. So nearly forever fallen, I didn't know if I were flying or still falling. He tossed me so I could rest on his shoulder and my neck almost snapped. Now I was right way up again and the epaulette on his uniform scratched my flesh. Was this really Smahil's pulse under mine?

He strode to the Prince and looked up at him.

'Why was I not told?'

'I saved her,' the Prince said at once. Misunderstood. Almost interested.

'Not *that* one,' Smahil ground his teeth, his voice vivid with contempt.

'But she's yours's sister.'

'Mine!' Smahil cradled me so possessively he nearly broke me. 'This is mine.'

'She,' the Prince pointed out in an It's-all-the-same-to-me way, 'is the accursed one.'

'Come with me. We'll escort her back to where they grabbed her. Gods! Why didn't I know, why didn't my bones tell me she was in the City?' He hadn't once yet spoken to me. I might have been a beloved statue. 'Does her mother know she's here?'

'Is her Mother – who I think her Mother is?' the Prince inquired guardedly.

'Very much so.'

'No, her Mother has no idea.'

'Where has she been living? Where?' And at last, to me, 'Cija, where have you been living?' When he spoke to me, his voice gentled. His voice was tender, and trembled;

he started to look into my eyes, but this was still too much for him.

'Come, Progdin,' he ordered.

'*He* is waiting for her, down there,' the Prince stirred himself to point one metal-dull arm.

I knew that Smahil, working with the Northerners as he is, for he has adopted their Army and risen to rank in it, in their plots with the spies of my father against my mother's régime – Smahil knows what they do not, that my terrible father is his also, though our mothers were indifferent.

Smahil's decision, after a pause, was complete.

'Kill the guards and leave no witnesses. Get the girls away like a miracle,' he said.

'As you will,' the Prince agreed, bored, and before he had finished speaking his blade had sheared off the head of the nearest ruffian. Smahil stabbed thrice more, and the sinewy top-soil was enriched. The Prince swung Bronza up before him. Smahil whistled. From a clump of trees trotted a docile male bird, seven feet high, beak like a sabre. Smahil and I mounted.

And now the bird and the hybrid pony made their confident way down between the shallow-bedded trees, down the face of the monstrous pyramid.

\*

At first Smahil held me so tight before him in the saddle, I thought I must bruise. He sensed my ache, and began to hold me as though I were eggs. If I leaned against his shoulder, I could see over it to the peak mounting ever higher up there, the flares doing nothing to illuminate that black crack that was to have been my doom. And by it, though I couldn't see them any more, lay the bodies of the Gurul-type thugs, who now could never explain the mystery of our escape.

'Lucky for you I happened to be passing just then,' Smahil remarked.

'How on earth did you recognise me in that dark, in the split-second they were going to throw me over?'

He was silent. Either he thought it was unnecessary to

repeat, or didn't want to admit, that he could recognise me any time, anywhere. Or he thought I was fishing for a compliment.

I wanted to tell him how recently he'd missed me by inches – in the jungle when he rode off after killing the ape-baby in my Tower, and rode right past me – rode off into the night with Urga.

As now he was riding off with me.

But I held back. I can't let him know his pet Urga's home is my home.

As the pyramid base widened nearer the sea from which it rose, the hillocks of earth and the undergrowth grew thicker and our mounts found the going much easier. There must even be water, pools pocked into the side of this man-made monstrosity. Frogs gurked and burped. Nocturnal waders, concerned with nocturnal worms, went Wicketty wicketty wicketty prrook prrook wicketty. If you looked down by the hooves of the pony in front, you saw the blinkless little eyes of nocturnal lizards – you could tell them from the diamonds in the pony's hooves, because those winked all the time.

'Progdin, have we time for a stop here?' Smahil yelled cheerfully, but still holding me more by magnetism than by touch, he was so delicate about it. 'Time to renew my acquaintance here.'

'I'll wait out of earshot, if you're both quick, if it's that urgent,' the Prince agreed indifferently.

'Ah, I daresay we can wait,' Smahil gaily about-faced. 'It's a muddy bed, after all, and she might not know which is me and which frogs. Besides, our friends on the jetty are ripe for visiting.

'How well do you know that girl in front?' Smahil asked me. 'I think I've a vague idea she's some sort of a relative to a girl I know.'

'I don't know her very well,' I was equally vague. 'She just happened to be walking along with me and so got into a very nasty incident. Thank you for getting us away.'

'You don't sound very overwhelmed to suddenly meet me.'

106

'I've known you are around. I've seen you a few times.'

'Sweet patient gods, why didn't you make yourself known?' Smahil checked his mount. 'Who are you with? Who's the fool you're living with who offers better protection – as we *see* – that you can't show yourself to me?'

'I'm not living with anyone else, Smahil.'

'What do you mean, you were "just walking" with this girl? Where were you "just walking"? What part of the City do you live in? Rather squalid, to judge by that elegant shift you're sporting. Well? Not that it matters. You'll be living with me from now on.'

'Smahil, that would be madness. You're working for the Northerners,' I added in a whisper, 'for our father. You're plotting, in fact, to overthrow my mother. What for? That way ambition lies? You're already the bosom companion of the Prince's nefarious amusements. Has our father recognised you?'

'He never knew I existed. Even my mother,' he said in the bitter voice in which he always speaks of her, 'shrugged me off into the world after marking me with her brand.'

'Well,' I said, 'someone recognised me all right. I was perfectly safe – and happy – till suddenly somehow word filtered through the back-alleys and up the back-waters to *him* that I was in his sprawling stink of a City.'

'No one will hurt you when you're with me. No one will know who you are.'

'They recognised me before.'

'Who?' Smahil demanded. 'Didn't *you* see anyone who could have recognised you?'

'Once – for three seconds – in the Palace – ' I said reluctantly.

'In the Palace? You get around, don't you? Who was it?'

'Snedde. My old nurse. But she wasn't sure. And then I got away quick. How could she be sure? Who would she tell?'

Smahil brushed a trailer of flower-bedewed air-root from my face.

'Snedde?' he said with slow distaste. 'Is that old woman your ex-nurse? Was she with you in that bloody tower?'

'Yes. But she never meant me any harm.'

'It needn't be she who meant the harm. Whoever she chattered to after she thought she saw you – Was . . . ' Smahil paused, then said, 'Was there a girl called Katisa – oh, you wouldn't know her name – a fair girl, a lady – with Snedde?'

'A fat little girl with curls? Yes, she was busy bosoming a letter and letting all the other girls know it was a terribly Top Secret love note.'

'It was,' Smahil said. 'From me.'

I felt winded. I hadn't known his taste was so sickly. Does Urga know he's got this other vulgar little noble-woman?

'Katisa,' Smahil explained, 'has been in a position for some while to notice and remark on the brand on my back. I haven't told her – much – but it's common gossip that these brands appear here and there on foster-children around the Court – people whose real Mothers are all rumoured to have been the silver-eyed witch Ooldra, curse her memory wherever her bones may be rotting. Katisa is a girl with a strong domestic sense. What she owns, she can't bear to lose – or to be threatened, not so much threatened in danger to itself, but threatened with loss from her possession. I can only suppose Snedde babbled to her about the brand you had from childhood, that marks you like me as a child of evil, the forbidden birth from the loins of a sacred celibacy. The mark that was set on us to show the devil his own. Katisa has heard me, sometimes, speak of my longing to see my sister again. I spoke so intensely that possibly' – Smahil smiled faintly – 'Katisa decided my longing was unhealthy. Anyway, she decided if my sister were about, my sister must remain unobtainable to me. She didn't want my attention elsewhere. She didn't want me ecstatic over another female, long-lost sister or not. When she heard from Snedde about the reappearance of the branded baby from the cursed Tower, Katisa put two and two together. She got word to the High Priest, who is known to have feelers out for this very reappearance. Deadly feelers. And the word spread, as you say, around the back-alleys and finally it crept along the river and found its way to the ears that are always waiting.'

*

Now we were on the landing-stage, that dubious point where the wavelets are neither salt nor fresh, where the river passes the pyramid-island and is sea.

There were flares, boats, more men.

'Dismount quietly here,' Progdin and Smahil whispered to Bronza and me.

We were obedient, and the men alone rode forward to the boat-guard who suspected nothing. Suddenly the two blades were out. There was slaughter. Shouting, confusion, torches swirling drunkenly, sparks spattering but unable to gain hold (we hoped) on the slippery wave-sloshed wood planks underfoot. The smell of blood more salt than the sea-smell.

Of course if the rescue were to be completed, these last witnesses must be killed as the others were by the high chasm. I had always known Smahil hesitates hardly a split-second before his frequent decisions to kill. There are very few whose right to live he respects. But the dark Prince too, whose ally's men these were, thought nothing at all of killing them. Of course these men are scum, rats, the priests' rats. But still they are planning with the Northerners for the Northerners' aims.

I turned in the shadow of the trees to Bronza.

'I'm taking one of these boats to get away unseen,' I said. I saw the whites of her eyes.

'Soppy,' she said. 'They'll see us safe to our door.'

'No. I'm afraid of the Major.'

'Perhaps you have your reasons,' Bronza conceded after a moment. 'I don't know, any more, what is sense and what isn't for you.'

'I owe you a long explanation – ' I said in a low voice. 'But now, Bronza love, I must get away. You stay. You have your lift safe home. You're O.K. They won't dream of hurting you. This is personal between the Major and myself.'

'I don't like you to go,' she said. 'Can you row? Can you find your own way back from the far bank? And, Cija, this current is strong.'

'I can look after myself fine,' I said. 'I'll see you in a couple of hours' time.'

'Best of luck –' she gave me a thumbs-up.

There was still a carnage on the landing-stage over there, men screaming, but there was no doubt at all who was in control. The pony and bird, both trained battle mounts, were kicking with horrible effect too. And the sounds, even the screams, didn't matter. The nearest bank was some miles away. Even if there were people on it (though it was not built on) and by a trick of wind they faintly heard the trouble, they'd never dare come over even if they had the means to do so. I hurried to the nearest moored boat. It was small and light and had two nice slim oars in the row-locks. Even though the current might do its worst with such a light boat, I decided I couldn't manoeuvre a heavier. I stepped in. I'm sorry, Smahil, I'm sorry, I kept thinking as I swiftly concentrated on undoing the rope and casting off. But I can't enter the nest of my enemies. And you and I, by reason of the bond between us, and what we have done, are fate's enemies. And within a month, within a week, shall I be alive if I come into your life with these plotters for my father and the Northern King? No, I would promptly have reaped the reward of the sin of being with you. I had to hurry. Already the sounds of slaughter were much, much less. The end was near. Another few minutes, and my desertion would be discovered before I'd had time to complete it. I hadn't even thanked him for saving my life, except in a surly way. He always gets me on the defensive, even when we haven't met for years.

The boat swayed and I nearly lost balance as the rope slid away.

I settled down on the plank-seat, and took hold of the oars. I passed Bronza, who waved intently, and then I passed Smahil's bird which was riderless and, immediately losing interest in the battle, unable to recognise opponents without his rider, had wandered back this way to snuff out lizards.

My heart missed beats. Was Smahil dead? I felt I must have killed him by sneaking away when I should have been watching to see he was not harmed. But then I saw him, on foot, the better to butcher the last wounded who had been trying to get into the water, though surely they wouldn't have lasted long enough to swim for it and spread their tidings. Smahil was leisurely, it never occurring to him I was not waiting under the trees.

I reached up to the creeper-snaky branches overhanging the glaucous water. I picked the biggest, lushest orchid I could make out. I reached out, the boat rocking most dangerously, and the bird, docile recognising me, came towards me, its beak and its claws black with thick blood. I stuck the flower into its bridle-strap, which was all I could reach, and hoped it wouldn't manage to chew it.

*

I was well away on the current when I heard the fury of the shouts from the little jetty. It was dark. I had a start, but best of all I was absolutely invisible only a few hundred yards away.

Bronza was right. The current was strong. But it was strong in the right direction.

Out here the river was far from quiet. There were alligators, not sleeping, barking. The sound carried and reverberated. It was very ugly. Every now and then there was a silver lightning as a fish leaped. Down below us, the boat and I, electric eels twisted full of poison. But there was no creaming of phosphorescence from my wake. Invisible.

*

Only one incident enlivened my journey back. I was relaxing, the trees of the far bank had slowly slowly become the trees of the near bank and were looming ahead. Suddenly I felt the most determined pressure on the boat, underneath. Oh *no*, I thought, furious with the river godlings for playing this trick, keeping the bad current till just the time

111

I sighted the end of the river-crossing. But it wasn't current. I bent over the side to see, as in vain I tried to fight the tug with the little oar-skill I have, and I saw an oily swelling and disturbance in the water. Then I saw the huge tentacle, shiny as glue, clamped by its blister-like sucker to the wood under-side of my boat. Panicky, I glanced over the other side. One tentacle suckered to us there, and one groping upwards, waving its tendrilly tip like a giant malignant sweet-pea. I bashed with my oar at the tentacle, which didn't register the blow except to quiver crossly. Then I felt the boat keeling. We were all out of true, the monster's grasp was tipping us over.

I'd have to swim for it. In that water! With that down there – and maybe some of its friends and relations! The whole black river boiling black, alive in every direction with tentacles and huge heaving slimy heaving wallowing bodies.

The boat tipped.

I could hardly get my footing. Any minute I'd be pitched out right into those waiting arms. I scrambled to my feet, put my hands together, and did a hasty dive. As soon as I hit the water – it was cold and heavy as oil – I knew I hadn't flung myself far enough.

I struck out, swimming as fast as I could, which meant awkwardly, with lots of splashing. The monster must be attracted by all this palaver I was making. Every moment I was sure I felt suckers on my legs, my hips, my breasts. Then another ghastly doubt occurred to me. Was I making in the right direction? I raised my head from the spray.

So black, everywhere. Was that trees over there? Or merely waves? Everything looked so different down here in the pursuing water.

I hurt my throat in order to look up at the stars. I'm no good at constellations. I'm no navigator. But as I looked up, hopelessly, I saw the tendrils above me. Cleaving the stars, waving gently – great tendrils directly above my head, curving down over my head.

I screamed and screamed. I screamed for Smahil, for my Gods, but without words. Then a great jolt knocked away

112

my breath, burning my lungs, from in front.

It has seized me.

I fought and twisted, hitting, flailing out at the waves. Then it struck me that I was not hitting anything more solid than water.

I paused. There was silence. My breath still burned from the blow. I was treading water. I looked up. Still there, the tendrils waved above me. They were foliage, the fan-leaves of gigantic ferns. I was directly against the bank. The blow on my chest had been the bank right in front of me. I had swum into it. Nearly knocked myself senseless. Nearly?

Too thankful to feel silly, I scrambled ashore.

Out there on the black river, my boat tossed unhurriedly, bottom end up, the little barnacles like settled moths.

The phosphorescent water ran off me like reluctant fire.

I turned inland. Now where was I? How wide was this strip of jungle I'd landed in? Which way was the City?

I felt bruised, aching, I had to touch my breasts not expecting them still to be whole and firm after that awful blow from the bank. But I was full of gladness and gratitude.

The jungle did not seem menacing. It lay bathed in a sweet dim light. It lay before me beckoning, little vistas opening up everywhichway. Now and then a leaf trembled, like a pulse from the jungle's tender heart. Trees seemed to be waterfalling out of the sky. There were creepers with flower-cups big as beakers, all folded for the night. There were trees on trees, air-trees thirty-five feet tall, balanced on boughs up there maybe a hundred and twenty feet or more. The air-trees' long thin roots dangled to the soil below, or to water, sipping it as through a straw. These long roots from the forest roof were all I saw that could be snakes. I couldn't feel nervous. I couldn't feel lost. I could feel nothing but this gladness.

Yet I knew this was land-outside-law, where live the murderers, the rapists, the keepers of private whipping-and-torturing establishments who can't afford the official rates, and the stealers of municipal railings for use as spears: all criminals who managed not to be arrested by the secular authorities till they were within the fifty acres of Temple grounds, and could therefore claim benefit of clergy, in which the Temple forcibly upheld them, jealous as the Temple is of the immunity of every fruit, hare and criminal on its land.

I wandered, moving like a glad dreamer. I walked straight through a hanging of lissom air-roots, and then I saw them all twitch and curl behind me. Still I knew they weren't hanging snakes, and I was right – I heard a sleepy scolding, and I looked up into a round gold eye, and there was a whole colony of monkeys nested up there in each other's arms, pillowed on each other's warm fur, with their silly tails (after a couple of safety-loops round the branch) hanging for anyone to pull.

I shall just wander, I said to myself. The jungle can't be very thick on this peninsula. I can't meet anything very terrible here, so near the City, and anyway it's such a friendly forest. When morning comes, I shall know my direction by the sounds of the workers coming to the fields.

I stopped to marvel at some toadstools. These growths were everywhere, but all different from each other. Every trunk seemed starred or beaded. There were toadstools swinging like stalactites, or pygmy bats, from the undersides of flower-wreathed boughs. There were fungi like tar-sludge, and others like poems of silver underwater bubbles.

I know what the forest here is like, I thought. It's like Atlan without Atlan's aloofness. It doesn't stand away and dare you to enter as Atlan does.

And at this moment I stepped out into a field, ranks of grain and wildflowers breathing fragrance to the stars, and there lay the City, spread out ahead like a valley of nightmares. I was sorry I'd found my way home.

*

Luckily I had only the Greens to go through, not the slums. The Greens aren't bad at night, maybe a bit of fornication under the trees or the stilts of some house, but none of that

114

danger teeming up and down the diseased alleys of the slums.

As I approached our house, I slowed my brisk pace through the dew. Bronza should be home by now. Would the dark Prince and Smahil be there too?

Our Green was marked by the hooves and claws that could mean only the Prince's pony and Smahil's Northern bird. But clearly, the tracks approached – and then left our house. Otherwise the Green was still thick with dew, so thick it was more like salt than crystal.

I hurried up the rickety steps.

The door had been left unlocked, so Bronza must be well in bed by now. There were wineglasses on the bench, but I didn't think Bronza could have invited our rescuers in – if she had given them wine, she would have washed up the glasses after, so as not to make Mother suspicious. The embers grunted low in the cavern of the hearth. I pulled off my sandals and almost flew up the stairs, and up again past the snores of the first landing, till I was in my cupboard under the eaves.

Seka was lying, fully-clothed, on my bed.

She was asleep, one side of her face fiery red where she had lain with her fist under it all night. She lay just the way she had been playing when sleep overtook her, her little buttocks up in the air, her hair curling damp simply from intensity. I was glad to see no tear-marks on her face. I wished whoever had put her in my room had also undressed her and put her in her crib. I tried to lift her without waking her – I must get a few hours' sleep in my own bed – but her eyes opened a slit and she gave me that bewildered look of a bruised flower uncertain as to which planet it had now wakened on. Her recognition of me on waking is always slow because she never accepts it at first. She has to keep on looking to make sure.

She was asleep again by the time I put her under her fleecy rugs, but she had made a little crooning sound. I am sure she will be able to talk again one day. She was even saying little baby sentences last year before the shock of the wormlarder made her dumb.

115

I noticed, as I drew the covers up and tucked her into a little private cocoon, that there was blood on her foot. I looked closer. It was a horrid mark, a deep bite. But she seemed not to have minded it, and it had at last stopped bleeding, though there was blood all over my coverlet, which at first I had not noticed, with my eyes unaccustomed to the room's gloom.

I went to the window. It had been left open. Perhaps one of those little blood-sucker bats had flown in for a snack. Seka will be O.K. – the bat's bite is soporific and can go unnoticed but for the long bleeding owing to the anti-coagulant in its saliva – but I'd better watch in case she develops anything, any fever or anything, infected by the little teeth. I had almost forgotten the stolen toys, and the ape-face at the window in the rafters above my bed, which had first made me vow never to leave the window open at night.

I leaned my arms on the sill. I could hardly believe there was still no sign of dawn in the sky. Or perhaps this was *tomorrow* night?

What a lot had happened. I pulled my shift over my head. I lay down under the blood-stiff coverlet. I was deathly tired, weighted as if by heavy water still. But my pulses beat and I needed Smahil, if I could have drawn him to my arms there would have been a dozen, a score of new sins committed that night in my narrow hard bed with the saggingstraw-stuffed pallet.

\*

Exactly one day later Urga informed us all that her Major was coming to share our evening meal – that very evening.

Mother clasped hands in delight. In fact, she nearly dropped Aega and the plant. (Her son Miyak, little fat daughter Aega and this plant she carried round with her in a clay pot, wherever she happens to be, from room to room to catch the sunlight, are the only things she never shows any affection for.)

Then she burst into a storm of abuse.

'Why the short notice? Couldn't we have *some* warning,

116

miss? Thoughtless slut! All right then. You do all the cooking and cleaning, it's all yours, I'll have nothing to do with it. As a matter of interest, do just tell me why in your opinion the Gods blessed you with a Mother. To slave, and agonise for you, and feed every layabout you choose to bring home?'

Urga stayed absolutely silent through all this, her head as usual now meekly bowed so that her lovely hair framed her face and hid her neck, on her face for a look of patient sweetness tinged with suffering.

As soon as the woman paused triumphant, Urga screamed at her mother, 'This was all your idea! You've made me nag and nag him to come home and meet you! I thought he'd come to loathe the very mention of my home! Now he's suddenly decided himself to honour us with a visit, and *he* chose tonight! This is all your pigeon.'

Her hair swung back. Her neck was stained purple, swollen. Mother stared at the revelation. She seemed to remember all her dreams of a daughter, mistress of a high ranking officer with generous ration allowances.

'We'll do our best,' she grumbled, 'in the time. Now get out. Buy me back pumpkins and stuffing and plenty of tender meats.'

'*We'll* spear you back a few dainty carcasses, eh, my boy?' said Father, shaving a finer point to his razor-sharp throwing-stick.

'If I have them by noon, that'll do,' Mother allowed.

And suddenly Mother was an animated duster-mop and Aega, probably for the first time since her birth, was told to finish feeding herself. She set up a malevolent Waaah and Seka stared at her with round eyes and then proudly set up a beastlier Waaah.

Father and Miyak grabbed up their weapons and got out fast.

Urga, behind Mother's back, sharply boxed Aega's ears. Aega shut up so Seka did too. I became aware that Seka's mouth was wide open and she was going Pup-pup – smacking her lips together with the round imperious eyes of an impatient baby nestling. I automatically began spooning breakfast into her.

Urga sat licking her milk and honey like a sleek half-grown kitten.

Bronza, troubled, drew me aside.

'I didn't tell the Prince nor the Major,' she said, 'that you live here, not even when the Prince had me on his pony before I realised you were going to take the boat to get away.'

'I expect he asked Urga outright if her mother has a lodger,' I muttered. 'Anyway, I shall quietly disappear long before he's due to arrive for our evening meal. If anyone notes my absence later, tell your Mother not to worry about me.'

Urga examined us over her honey-spoon. A crease appeared between her brows. She was used to sharing secrets with Bronza, not to Bronza drawing anyone else aside, and she must have felt something askew in her world.

'Aren't you looking forward to his visit?' she asked. 'He's fairly easy to be with once you can take his sarcasm. He's nice with me at least. He says I'm the only girl he's ever been able to talk properly to.'

*

Afternoon, and Mother staring discontentedly around.

'It's cleaner now,' she grumped. 'But it needs class.'

'Oh, Mother, he doesn't expect us to be a mansion.'

'Look at all those stags' scowls with splendid antlers on the wall, Mother. That's mute evidence of our ancestors' prowess, even if Father did buy them as a job lot.'

'We need a bit of *status*,' Mother chewed her lip.

And she sent Urga over to Ogdrud's to borrow Ogdrud's parrot (with its perch) to add a splash of colour to our interior decoration.

Splash is only too right. The parrot is a macaw, and not house-trained. It boasts gaudy gold and purple feathers, an unlovely beak which seems encrusted with unhealthy growths, and a street-cry voice. Mother surveyed it proudly.

118

'He won't be shocked by its swearing, will he?' she said.

Now they were satisfied with the place, and the smells of the meats and marrows in Mother's pots and cauldrons were getting pungent, they were all off upstairs to decide which beads and which dresses. And it was time for me to make my slinky getaway.

But I kept leaving it till a little later, because I couldn't leave Seka alone for hours while no one was downstairs with her – and then Miyak and Father trudged in from the Hunt with a few rodent corpses and dead lizards no one wanted now, and I had to serve them a hasty meal because they said they were starving and couldn't wait till the big meal.

And then suddenly, one and a half hours early when I still thought I had plenty of leeway, that old familiar Northern sound of trampling claws outside stopped my heart, and came close, and there was a bit of jingling and a harsh bird-bark (that set the macaw cursing blue murder), and then a heavy clap-clap on the door, like an order, made with Smahil's iron-banded gauntlets.

I stood petrified. I was paralysed with horror. There is no back door out of any of these houses, simple structures of wooden boxes set on each other like a child's game with a few stairs rearing up the centre.

I hadn't even got myself looking decent. I'd never thought Smahil would arrive before he'd said. But he knows the workings of my mind better than I'll ever know his.

'Go on, then,' Mother hissed and gave Urga a shove.

Urga skidded to the door. She was as flushed as her neck. Her violet eyes were huge. She looked terrified, and awed.

She opened the door. In an odd constricted hostess-voice, she chirped, '*Ah* – hello – ' as if he were the last thing she'd expected to find on the step.

'My man is tying my bird to one of your stilts,' Smahil said.

'Fine,' Urga said with enthusiasm. I don't think any of us had expected the 'man'. He was a batman-groom, I suppose, but not in uniform. And he was so young, so

119

graceful in his melodramatic livery of velvet the blue of an Admiral's eyes with places like bruises squashed into it where the velvet had marked.

I looked rather narrowly at him to make sure he wasn't a sweet little transvestite. I haven't forgotten my own days of employment as a page with a draughty doublet.

Smahil stepped in past Urga.

'*Do* come in,' Urga said.

His eyes moved gravely to us without pausing on any one of us. I had stopped halfway to the stairs, holding Seka. I couldn't get past Father and Miyak without pushing them.

'Which is your Mother?' he asked Urga.

Urga introduced him to Mother, who bridled at the compliment of being judged indistinguishable from us. She's handsome of course, and prow-breasted, but looks her years.

'I trust you will be kind enough to accept this small rather unworthy token of my gratitude tonight for your generous invitation,' bowed the self-appointed guest.

His page staggered up to Mother and unloaded on to her an elephantine curving gilded wicker cornucopia of jewel-bright wines in glass, and spices, and smoked meats, and even two valuable canisters of salt, which was a courteous thought and would help make up for tonight's spread which this household can ill afford.

'And look,' said Mother, pulling out packages and watching something like brown sand pour out of one: 'Sugar – that's the sweetener rich people use instead of honey, isn't it – ?'

'Come and say hello to my Father – my sister – or Cija – my brother,' Urga said, tagging Miyak on as an afterthought.

I was holding Seka, who was filthy because she'd been allowed to play in the mud under the house while everyone was so busy. My hair was all over the place, I hadn't combed it since dawn. My hands were wet, and the sleeves of my old shift pushed up because I'd been scrubbing.

Smahil took my wet hand to greet me, but let it drop rather obviously and with an expression of the politest disdain. To the whole household he was subtly insulting, I

120

thought, being *too* civil and equal to show how careful he was being not to show he was slumming.

He looked with sudden keenness at the child perched regarding him from my arms. He hadn't been told about her. He wasn't sure if I were a mother.

'I see I came a little before time?' he raised his brows at me.

'Yes,' I agreed but Mother drowned me out – 'No, no, Major. How we've been looking forward to this occasion, you simply can't conceive, Major!'

She made frantic gestures for another stool to be found. She hoped the meal would go round now this page was here too.

Greeting Miyak, Smahil's face hardened. He looked like white stone, or worse, steel. Fine upstanding virile lad, he was thinking.

Let him. Why should he be told, if he can't see for himself, that Miyak is as callow as they come? One of those awkward hobbledehoys that think every new female under the age of, well, fifty is the most enchanting creature walking the Gods' earth. He did indeed at one time think that I was the sweetest purest most romantically shop-soiled damsel in distress, but he's since met at least two thousand other females (or at least pinched them in a crowd) and each of those in turn has been the sweetest, or naughtiest, or prettiest, or most bewitchingly ugly, or even the most fascinatingly plain girl in the entire world.

Smahil had become stern, as if displeased. Mother hastened to trundle in her unready meal.

Father ordered Miyak to draw up the settles, and we all plonked down around the groaning board.

Fernak the young wolf skulked in a corner. I held Seka, Mother held Aega whose fingers were instantly in Smahil's food, and the macaw did idiotic somersaults on its perch.

'Wine, Major?'

Smahil waved away the proffered root-fermentation. 'A little of the dry red I brought, I think,' he said.

'Magnificent cook, yours,' Smahil then said, spreading a little sweetness and light.

Mother simpered. 'I am responsible for all my own cooking,' she revealed.

The stuffed marrows were still a trifle raw, but aromatic. But there was verdigris on the 'company' cutlery. Verdigris-splotched knife-blades, and spoons and skewers in warped handles that had grown too loose. I looked round our room that already smelt of parrot. Every mirror is flyspotted, every mug cracked, every drawer minus a handle.

Smahil asked for a second helping.

'You like it?' Father boomed. 'Ah, yes, this is real home-grown food going down you, my boy.' (Urga was agonised. A Hunter can't call a Major 'my boy'.) 'You know all the ground in our bit of yard is rich as plum-pudding? Fertilise it myself.'

'Indeed, sir?' Smahil raised fascinated brows.

'My own compost heap down there,' Father went on, pleased. 'It's amazing what you can do with organic rot.' (Father loves this phrase, 'organic rot'. Smahil's gaze wandered towards mine across the table, away, to mine – and held on mine. I couldn't read his expression but it was darkling, imperious, and I tore mine away with an effort. Smahil's nostrils flared wide and dilated.) 'You know we're eating my old leather jacket now?' Father chuckled. 'My old jerkin, rotted away with the fishbones and, well, so on, that make my cabbages best-in-Greens.' (He thumped the table. The wine-jugs jumped and leaked.) 'You know, I found a dead cat the other day –'

Mother and her children were crimson.

The page picked his nails with precision. Haughtily he pushed his plate away, wouldn't eat any more.

A boot touched my foot under the table. I looked up, startled. Smahil smiled. Grimly. No escape, his smile mocked. But there was that brooding fury behind the mockery.

I drew my foot in, under my chair, out of reach. I remembered the things I had remembered last night. My thighs throbbed. The pulse in my groin must have beat blue.

(Urga began to sparkle. Perhaps it was her foot now.)

I suffered the keenest pleasure just looking at Smahil, not even looking at him, just being across from him. The ache of years began to melt. I felt a dozen loads lighter.

'Do you find our City much changed after your sojourn in the Northkingdom, Major?' Mother steered the conversation to intellectual channels.

'Unchanged, madam.' Again the slight pressure on my pursued foot. 'Still in ruins, raddled with disease.'

Mother sallowed to her hair-roots.

'Major! You can't forget how our land has suffered.'

'Our Dictatress has not a very extensive rebuilding project, has she?' Smahil swilled his mouth with his own wine.

'Even the few buildings which were stone in bygone days, have been rebuilt thatch and wattle – if they have been rebuilt. Just what do all these new taxes go on? Even rat-traps are taxed. Can't she afford architects better-trained than latrine-diggers?'

'It's just possible she has other things to think of,' I said. 'One or two little plots afoot for the overthrow of her dynastic rule, a spirit of insurrection rampant simply for insurrection's sake, so obviously an excellent reason for insurrection, a few worthy folk bending their genius to her assassination.'

The table looked oddly at me. Bronza looked alert. Smahil's nose lengthened in a sardonic sneer.

'No dynasty should last too long. It begins to moulder,' he said. He looked straight at me. 'And in-breed,' he said with superb distaste.

'But our Dictatress has fought with all she's got, with every ounce of her strength, to beat back the invader,' Mother said. I warmed to her.

'And still the ravens flap and feast on the gibbets.' Father sighed, doubtless thinking of all that wasted on ravens. 'We've been invaded too often.'

'Perhaps, then, a new régime with a ruler who made a pact with the invaders would be healthier for the country,' the boy Miyak suggested.

Smahil looked thoughtfully at him.

'Miyak!' the sisters cried. 'They should have left you on

that rack. That's treachery, poltroon, beneath contempt, denial of every moment of the thousands of years of our heritage.'

'Tough,' Miyak muttered.

'I don't like this Northern Army over-running our streets,' Mother said. 'Oh, Major, I know they're your adopted Army. I know they're supposed to be friendly. But you mark a silly woman's words, within months there'll be Troubles. And then it'll all be to do over again, the would-be conquerors, the broken heads on the cobbles, the treachery in high places, the soft words, the looting and raping and burning, and the torture of children.'

'And it'll be the day of the Dragon again,' Urga said.

An electric stab went through me at the mention of my husband. I felt Smahil's eyes on me. I felt the old sick hatred of the dark conqueror whose dark throne and darker bed I have shared beyond the turmoiling ocean.

Mother squealed.

There was a flop flop sound from under the table. The toad that lives under our water-butt had decided on one of its visits.

The toad, coruscated like a bit of far-gone fungus or a miniature Ael, in a series of mobile squats made it to the hearth. The macaw heaped contumely on its head and jumped up and down. The toad swivelled one eye in its socket to look up at the macaw. That quelled it. The toad wallowed before the fire, basking in the comfortable rage of the flames.

'Shoo, shoo! Hideous thing! Ech!'

Mother assaulted the toad with the broomstick from the corner.

The toad swelled. It started burping noises like ghastly indigestion, stating its territorial rights.

Mother prised its green backside off the warm stone flags. With a filthy look at her, the toad fouled the floor. It then conceded the battle, flopped away to the door. Mother's bosom set the low-cut gown dancing. Shame heaped on shame.

As the toad queased down over the step, a knock

sounded on the open door. The macaw swooped on the toad, no longer formidable in retreat, and triumphantly speared it in spite of a neat spit in the eye from the toad. Fernak paced across and took the feasting macaw in his jaws. 'If that's some neighbour, ask them when was the law passed that decent folks can't dine in privacy.' Mother snapped.

I crossed the room and went into the kitchen to open the door.

I expected to see Ogdrud asking should he feed his parrot with his special seeds, and expecting to be asked in.

Instead a wave of expensive perfume wrenched from the genitals of the stags and the glands of civet hit and wound around me.

Festooned with fur, a boa of the joined tails of little dead animals, a young woman stood trembling on the step in the gloaming. I couldn't remember wherever I'd seen her before. She had beseeching blueish eyes, and a nose all tilt. She was pretty.

She was the lady Katisa. 'You are the lady Katisa,' I informed her.

'How do you know? Is the Major with fair hair here? I have a message for him. Is he here?'

She wasn't sure.

She'd traced him, followed him. She was suspicious. Of the white-haired pauper Urga. Or of the new-found sister rumoured to be floating around somewhere within the City. Or just suspicious. But she wasn't sure, was he here?

'He's here,' I said. 'Come in.'

The beseeching look left her eyes. She'd won. She shushed into the kitchen. Now she was mistress of the situation. The big shabby kitchen dwindled and dingied around her. She smelt expensive, she was all fur and pearls and she didn't look so much clean, as groomed – her nails each pointed to the same shape, her face powdered and rouged to the delicacy of a tearose, the lobes of her little ears discreetly rouged and sequins sprinkled inside them, her brows plucked even more carefully than mine in the brothel. She was pretty.

125

'He's in that room,' I said.

I hardly had time to stand politely aside. She arrowed in.

She didn't suspect me of a thing. Whoever she believed Smahil to be visiting, it wouldn't be a poor creature with dishevelled hair and a most inedifying shift.

The faces turned to her.

Smahil's brows clenched fractionally before they went right up. 'Katisa, my dear. Why this intrusion?' he quite baldly said.

'You were seeing me tonight, Smahil.'

'You mistook the time, Katisa. Or I did.'

'You can't dismiss me so, don't think it, my lord.'

Surely *now* he must see her softness, her sickliness, all that groomed matt finish with its deadness sleep-walking, the zombie 'delicately reared' girl wakened to a grabbing semi-life, excited by and lusting after the new shaft of oxygen, the first man she's seized who is vividly alive and out of her twittery world, but whom she is making every effort softly to strangle.

Why am I so nasty about her? Oh, perhaps, yes. She reminds me of Lara, my husband's second wife.

Well, does Smahil still think this soft meat enchanting now he sees her beside Urga? Nerves have brought Urga's firm little chin up in rosy spots, and her legs are still coltishly knock-kneed, but otherwise she's slim and vital with a head of rippling flame, white-hot, and she looks so full of health and sweetness you could turn her inside out and still not have all the sweetness sucked out, and she can whistle a pornographic song through two grubby agile fingers, or shin up a tree the roughed noble-woman wouldn't even see as she passed it.

'I'll bring in the pie,' I said, and I closed the kitchen door behind me.

I'm well out of it all. He's not tossing me back in. He's not having me again, driving me mad with this and that. He has no right to me.

The eyes of the freak potatoes ranged along the kitchen mantel watched me.

I opened the door. I stepped out into the twilight. I

126

pressed my hand to my brow. I couldn't think.

Smahil has come for me. Smahil wants me. But is it to devour me? He is determined to have me. That, as he sees it, is quite simply fate. There will never in his concept be any future for me but Smahil. Smahil will devour me. If he could do nothing else with me, he would eat me. I think I quite believe that.

A mist was spiralling up, a drizzle spidering down. The drizzle shone like coloured needles, quick dainty-fingered skilful flashes, from this angle or that, as the house-lamps lit them. A kinkajou laughed and scampered from one smocked thatched roof to another.

Three steps or so I journeyed into the twilit rain. Mother's herbs rustled around my hem, fragrant, feathering their wet tickling heads against my ankles and up under my shift.

Blanked out in the dark, I saw I was outside the square of gold window. Inside the big room, Miyak and Father waited for Cija to bring in their hot sludgy succulent pie, Fernak with feathers like toothpicks protruding from his snout twitched his strong tail, Smahil's page looked ill, little Seka waited in my chair (I'm never leaving my baby again), Mother and the girls took it all in as Smahil, lounging back against the rush-weave settle, taunted Katisa whose plump fists I could see curling like her hair. The raindrops slid against the glass, contorting, dazzling. I couldn't hear any of it. But I felt completely outside the scene. Anyway, I turned to go back in. And like a bolt from the sky, two incredibly strong arms seized me from behind and swung me up, like flying, into the little gourd-tree and thence up on to the damp squelchy fibrous thatch, and thence to a great arching tree. All before I could catch my breath.

Only now was I able to scream.

But a hand clamped my mouth. And again I was swung up, and again, and we were amongst the trees, the strip of jungle that watches the Greens.

But we were high, amongst these wet high trees.

I lay still, as I had been thrown, over some great creature's back. The breath had been knocked from me.

127

Was this some new scheme of my father's to kidnap me? But the hand, the hand that had instantly choked my scream. Like iron it had been, or like part of a tree – hard and ungiving as bark, yet as texturous too.

I explored, with such senses as I had left, the back against which I lay inert as we travelled at this terrible rate through the boughs and branches.

Some huge being had me over his shoulder. Clothed in very thick coarse bearskin, or wolf-skin – or naked, and naturally hairy. The boughs bent and swayed. The little silver rains rained. Now there were star-needles. We were that high. An ape! One of the huge apes had cast an eye on me, like the one visitant at my window, and now was swinging me off to its lair – or larder.

I screamed, but the thick coarse hair against my face muffled my scream. I beat my fists, I struggled, I kicked, I tried to kick myself free at the risk of falling over a hundred feet to the forest floor. But still I was borne effortlessly into the night black of the chirruping, barking, howling, rustling, slithering jungle.

# PART FOUR
## THE APES' ARENA

So here I was.

Wherever here might be.

My back against a hard solid stone wall, though after all that nightmare through the trees I could hardly believe anything was solid. There were snores all around me but no bribe in the world – except safety – could have sent me off to sleep. I could only wait till light to show me where I was, and what, dear God, I was among. Once I started stealthily to inch forward. I'd got hardly three inches, before a huge hand vised my ankle and dragged me inexorably back, grazing my shin on the stone. The next time I was allowed to get a couple of yards, but it was only 'allowed'. There was a chuckle as I was dragged back this time, and the longer way back was more painful.

I sat amongst the smells and snores. The smell was very strong, bestial. The chuckle, as I reheard and reheard it inside my head, was amused but, I was sure, non-human. There was something just off-key about it. It had been too rich, too low, yet too big.

I joggled my tongue in the space where I had lost a side tooth a long, long time ago in Southerncity. I prayed.

Dawn leaked into the sky. I realised the stars had gone out, then that it was lighter anyway. The first things I began to make out were pale splotches high up in the sky. Slowly, as the light grew, uneven triangles widened down from the splotches. I understood. I was seeing mountains. The splotches were snow peaks. They splayed floated on mauve, mauve airs lightening slowly, slowly.

Something seemed familiar about these splotches, as I gazed on them, because the urgent important scene about me was still in darkness.

129

First a huge conical mountain seemed about to crash down right plummeting upon us, then another a little way behind it all chasms and cliffs edged by far lightnings, and thunders we could not here hear toppling tiny distant slow-motion boulders big as castles, and again beyond both, a third mountain, that floated in its own haze, wreathed like a crone-goddess in shifting veils of fogs that passed at the pace of a mile a day.

These were the mountains of my infancy.

These were my only 'outside world' till I had weathered seventeen years.

The sky lightened slowly. Yellow it grew, and a bird threw a thin high song to the sky, and the nearest mountain spooled it back in a thread of bat-song.

There rose the mountains I had watched from my Tower, and here I was, in my Tower, in the courtyard with its dry fountain, and all about me snored the tribe, the ape-men, their great hair-sleeked muscles bulging even in their roaring sleep, their tusks shining in rows. There must be twelve full-grown bulls in the tribe, as I counted them now, maybe twice as many females, and quite a number of small ones, and tiny wrinkled bornings with their sleeping lips suckered in tubes clamped to their sleeping mothers' long nipples protruding like rubbery thumbs from the matted wealth of crimson hair.

I moved quietly to the parapet and looked over. Hopelessly steep as when I was a child. And as I turned, I saw fixed sleepless on me the glowing gaze, like two hot coals, of my guard – my captor?

First one ape awoke, then another yawned as its great beetle-browed head shifted off its mighty chest, and it cracked its joints and reached forward and picked a bone or a busy dung-beetle from the excreta-soft odorous dust of the courtyard, and began to chew.

Presently they were all awake.

The females crowded round me. They pinched my arms and stared intently, stooping, into my face. They grumbled gutturally to each other. My guard kept them from handling me too much. One big cow got a little rough with me: my guard cuffed her lightly and she retreated with a matter-of-fact snarl.

I pieced it all together and began to realise why it was only the females crowded around, while the males squatted apart, chewing their beetles.

I was fodder. But as yet I was fit only to be part of their larder. I was not plump enough. I was no good to the tribe as I was. The babies would not get enough nourishment from me as I was.

So now they all scattered, and when they came back, for every grub or beetle that they popped into their own mouths, they came up trying to force one into my mouth.

I kept shaking my head and making piteous sounds of protest. They were puzzled, but simply decided I didn't know how to crack the beetles' carapaces for myself. They did it for me, shoved a couple in their own mouths and exaggeratedly rolled their eyes and Yum-yummed their lips to show me how delicious it was, then thrust more at me. I shut my mouth tight and my guard reached forward and wiped the crushed grubs off my face and proffered them again to me, but I made a face of distaste.

As the day wore on, I would have given a lot for a few juicy larvae or pupae, but I was also determined to starve myself to death rather than fatten up and let them pronounce me ready to be torn apart and fed to their toothless infants.

The males lumbered to their long flexible feet and one by one swung into the overhanging trees and made off in a troop till the jungle swallowed them.

Throughout the day the females kept coming up with daintier and juicier looking morsels. They even came with bananas and fat berries they must have meant to keep themselves. But though my belly felt hollow as a stretched drum, I wouldn't eat. I hoped they'd decide I was useless, and let me go.

Finally my guard lost patience. He seized my head in one hand – his hairless but clammy palm curved right round my head – and forced back my jaw. With the other hand

131

he crammed a fistful of squirming grubs into my mouth. I wasn't quick enough to spit all of them out, and he'd crammed them so far back I swallowed some before I was aware. I gagged and choked but I felt better. It's only like swallowing oysters, I told myself.

As the little ones became sleepier, and stopped gambolling and climbed into their mothers' fur, and the heavy orchids rioting on the old walls closed for the evening on the buzzing flies and bees on the rapine among their pistils, and I dazedly wondered how many more days, or how few, I had left like this one, the bulls returned, swinging twenty feet at a time from the nearest branches to the plinth of the balustrade.

They bore effortlessly on their shoulders rodents, and a couple of deer, with great holes torn in their throats, and their necks twisted nearly free of their still warm bodies. The apes had no weapons I could see, only their huge fangs and their tusks and their great hands with stabbing nails broad as small saws, yet they had overpowered even a stag with a five-foot spread of shining antler.

The males dumped their catch down in the dust. The females and young gathered around, grunting and drooling, but they did not dare to move in till the males had had their fill, roasting hunks and offal spitted with sharp sticks and thrust crackling and spitting in the fire the females keep always burning down under the old dry well-hood, out of the wind and weather.

My guard was shifting and grunting. He had spent all day watching me, instead of off in the trees on the hunt with the other bulls, and now he was not included in their meal either. Suddenly he made his decision. He looked at me, moved over to the feast, looked again at me, came back and gave me a terrible cuffing which knocked me to my face in the dust, and meant, You stay there as no uncertain warning – and he lolloped over to the fire.

Three of the bulls looked up. I thought they were going to contest the non-hunter's right to part of the day's catch. But they snarled and pointed at me. They didn't want me left to my own devices. I am ear-marked for their young,

132

the coming generation of their tribe. Presumably to them, two-legged and two-handed as I am, escape by a twenty-foot jump is as thinkable for me as for themselves.

The bulls jabbered. The one who had guarded me was giving cavernous resonant belches, presumably to show how empty he was. I knew how he felt. Then one of the younger leaner bulls looked across at me from under the cliff-bar of his red brow. He came shambling across to me on his knuckles, pulling with him a leg of roast. He was going to take the other's place as a show of fair play – for a while.

He squatted there beside me, hunkering on his hairy, powerful legs, tearing pieces off the stag-leg. Finally he looked aside at me. He thrust the leg at me. The hoof still glistened on the end of it, delicately cloven, so recently bounding across valleys and streams through sweet grass.

At the thought even of that sweet grass my stomach turned over. I wouldn't look at the roast after the first glance. But the male must have seen the longing in my eyes as I turned away. Slowly and tantalisingly the roast was passed before my eyes, before my nose and mouth. Then the ape chuckled and applied himself to it.

My guard had gorged himself by the fire. Now he shambled back to me, and the younger male swung away.

Stars came out over my old Tower. The apes grunted and folded themselves into corners. In a circle, with their backs to the hot stone of the well with the fire ever flickering in it, crouched the four biggest bulls. They were so muscularly obese that it was hard to tell, in this light, whether they were females with dewlapping chests. But when a half-grown bull tried to squat against the hot stone, an immense bull with fire-jewelled tusks gave a bellow and staggered upright, a difficult posture for an older male top-heavy with muscle, but so awe-inspiring that his right to his chosen territory was established without more ado, and the young one slunk away to copulate sulkily.

The next afternoon I was weak with hunger.

I wondered whether I could eat a little one day, and nothing the next, and keep unappetising enough that way.

Or if they'd give me up as hopeless fattening-wise, yet not hopeless bony, better than nothing, and just rend me without warning.

A commotion below the Tower sent all the females, toting young, to peer over the parapet.

My big grey guard cuffed me when I even turned my head that way. But when he decided he wanted to look too he yanked me to my feet and hauled me over behind him. Thrusting with his free arm, he made the females draw aside for him. He (and I, perforce) looked down on a dreadful scene while the females chattered and honked at our shoulders.

A mastodon was being driven against the Tower wall by the males, who must have sprung it in the jungle and herded it here by degrees, maybe for hours. The mastodon kept standing at bay, or lowering its head and sweeping in unexpected directions, its immensely live trunk was the savage sensitive intimate pink tip questing, its tusks shearing.

I thought it had already taken one victim, as there were fewer bulls below.

As I watched, another ape was pierced by a razor-tip of ivory. Blood spouted. His fellows hesitated as he spun in agony, clutching his ruined belly. I thought they meant to help him, till one darted in and sunk its fangs in the wounded one's wound. The wounded one tossed and began high screams. I couldn't understand what was happening till I realised the other ape was tearing away at the wound, drinking the life-giving blood. The other apes down there (and up here) looked as if they'd like to rush and join in but the mastodon was charging again. First things first. Steadily, with only their voices (reverberant as boat-horns) and their darting presence at every turn, throwing heavy boulders in the giant's eyes (it was streaming blood) and jabbing sharp stones at its flank from all sides, bewildering and dooming the mastodon, steadily they backed it till with a crash (I expected the Tower to topple) the mastodon seemed to go right through the ground, as in fact it had done, and into a cleverly camouflaged pit.

Now, trumpeting and screaming hysterically, so I thought my eardrums and my heart would burst at the dreadful sounds of pain and rage, the mastodon tried vainly to struggle out. One side, in fact, was the sheer wall of the Tower. They had it. Dancing round it with boasting, purposeful glee, the apes rained boulders and stones upon it, and presently signalled up to us, whereupon a female seized a brand from the fire-well. She tossed it down to them, where it fell with an anaconda hiss in the mastodon's bed of fern and foliage. Immediately twenty other flames had sprung from that one, and the mastodon shrieked and tossed so I could feel the Tower shake, as it began to roast alive.

*

By evening, as the bats whined overhead and the hunting owls were out patrolling for prey, the monster in the pit was still.

The flames had died down. Now only a smoke hung about the brown new edges of the pit, and a smell of charred hair and hide and blackened ivory that had been noble. And an undeniable fragrance.

The bulls again approached the pit. They bounded down into it. They tore with stones, with sharp old bones, at the murdered mastodon's hide, and presently the vast cage of gleaming ribs were bared, and the heart a huge red rawness still with a throb in it.

The females gathered their young to them. They swung out over the parapet, leaping for the trees, bounding down to the feast.

My guard dithered. He glared at me. Finally he pointed to the nearest tree, then at me, then back to the tree.

'Thanks for the invitation,' I said. 'If you leave me up here, you'll find me obediently waiting your return. I can't jump those distances.'

'Urgulgringlechech,' he said moodily.

Suddenly he grabbed me up, tossed me over one shoulder and made off with me.

As my head hit against his shoulder-blade and nearly

lost me another tooth, my heart thumped with a wary, panicky joy.

At least down here I could make some sort of a dash for it, even if it only set the whole tribe after me, precipitating the end.

After a breathless drop, I was laid on the turf. I was out of that hateful Tower. I wheezed and gasped, fighting like a drowner for a return of breath.

Now my huge grey guard again wanted to dive into the mastodon for his share. The poor giant burned corpse was crawling: bulls, females, little ones were crawling through the arches of the ribs, across the cave-like pelvis, fighting each other for the prizes.

There was not much blood left, though these creatures seem to go quite crazed by the sight of spouting blood, which I suppose they believe is a life-force and marvellously magically beneficial to the drinker – actually I suppose it is pretty full of protein. But the brutes kept up a continuous snarling, and were so busy claiming and protecting choice morsels they hardly had time to enjoy them, and bolted them down so no one else could grab them. Great greasy apes, rolling in ponds of gravy, flew at each other's throats in contest for the most intrinsically symbolic of the mastodon's attributes: the red heart, the grey creamy brain, the incredible testicles, the mountain of viscera. The females and young crawled like contented hyenas around the edges, darting up a tunnel of ribs to seize some dainty as its owner left it in order to defend it from a rival bull.

My grey guard grew restive. Finally he couldn't bear it. He pretended I no longer existed, a neat solution, and took a header into the pit.

I moved cautiously at first, as though I weren't moving at all. Then I saw no one, not even some old spiteful female, was looking my way.

I ran.

Oh my little dear and private God, how I ran! I was within the blessed shade of the trees. And a flying tackle from behind brought me down. I lay full-length on the springy forest floor, too weary even to look at my conqueror. And I heard the low heavy rich chuckle I had heard in the night. It was not my grey guard. it was the younger wirier male, the crimson male.

He wouldn't lift me. He stood over me and jerked with his hands till, tottering, I stood. He must enjoy taunting the poor white hairless female they were keeping for the toothless infants. If they even recognised me as a female – their own being so different.

Now he clamped an arm about my shoulders, in a grip that bowed me nearly double and smeared me with blood and mastodon-grease – and walked me deliberately back to the pit.

'Huah!' he stood and roared.

The grey guard's head rose from the mastodon's entrails.

The crimson male pointed at me, then, derisively, at the guard. He was calling insults. The others even paused to watch.

The grey guard was above insults now. He was handling the last prize left, the huge spongy seed-bag.

Before he could sink his teeth in an ecstatic bite, the crimson ape had leaped in straight upon him, seized the bag, taken a great bite in token of ownership, and hurled the bag away.

Obviously the grey guard, inefficient and impassive when berated, niggled him.

But now at last the grey guard was roused. That had been a tidbit that really was a status symbol. Giving a sudden roar with a shriek in it too, he turned like a rattler and sunk his great teeth in the crimson shoulder.

The crimson ape was younger and fractionally less heavy. The teeth in his shoulder were shaking him to and fro. It must have felt like being in the jaws of a hippopotamus. But he twisted free and brought up one of his legs (a human being could never have done it) and placed his foot, with its prehensile thumb-like big toe, full in the offending face. And dug in, black talons and all.

The grey guard screamed his rage. He spat and gibbered,

his hold broken, and returned to the fight in a battering rush.

Locked, writhing, swayed the two apes. The tribe jabbered.

With a heave, the grey had the red's head in his hand, hairy fingers spread all over it like the legs of some middle-aged tarantula. And the grey proceeded to force the red, by pressure on his near-snapping neck, till he was right before one of the mastodon's tusks. Back, back, the grey forced the red. He was going to spike him on one of the points!

Now the attention of the entire tribe was focused.

My guards were about to kill each other. I turned. But I was hemmed in by females. The red had placed me well. If I moved, they moved too, not looking at me, staring at the fight but nudging me back into line.

The red ape in the pit lunged as the point behind him was about to impale him. With abhuman ferocity he hurled the grey to the floor of the mastodon grave. It was over in seconds. The red drank blood from the grey's throat, severing the jugular vein, while the grey, momently still alive, rolled its offended flat eyes. Then there was no sound but the gargling of the victor. And the screams and bellows of the previous minutes died in our ears.

That night, as we all returned to the Tower, laden with chunks of half-burnt mastodon, there seemed quite a party spirit.

One female lay out, spread-eagled, in a corner of the parapet. She was grey with approaching senility, probably all of twenty-six years old, with a suppurating jaw where some old blow had festered never healing, and her stomach protruded like a third breast, the navel long and pointed as a third nipple (I suppose, if their mothers don't bite the cord off at the birth, it's left till it withers and just flakes off in the winds.) I thought she was resting after gorging herself. Then one male after another shambled up, mounted and entered her. Soon there was a queue of males, grunting, waiting their turn.

She lay, passively, her eyes closed, only her matted

bowed thighs open, as though dissociating herself from the entire incident. And yet other females were moving around unmolested, or giving meekly in to one male only, waiting patiently till he withdrew, and then moving off to their young again. Why had this one invited what seemed no pleasure, or even no interest, to her? Or had she invited it? Perhaps she had just realised it was inevitable. I understood. She was the grey guard's female, and now that the red conqueror had mounted her once, just for the sake of form, then signified that he was not claiming her as part of his harem, she was anybody's. There were more than enough females for everybody, but they belonged to the bigger bulls, and there were younger bulls who had to sneak what they could get when the big ones were otherwise occupied. The females didn't seem to care who it was, their master or an interloper; they simply waited, then moved on.

Females, however, could not be very important in this social system. An olding one like this, at any rate, was discarded by the young red, though he could have started a harem with her and risen in status. But perhaps she was past the age of child-bearing, and only ate up food, and was nearing the age when she'd be left out on some hill-top, or in some glade, or in the mouth of some cave, to propitiate the forest-demons, or the cave-bear, or the eternally hungry sabred tiger.

I thought this must be the tribe's solution to old age, unless they ate them. There were no ancients.

I knew I was not in any dangers lesser than death. They can't see me as female. I am clothed, so perhaps they think I am a male, or a neuter of my kind. I am so pale, and puny, and bare of hair, I must seem repulsive as a slug, fit only for eating.

The night beat down on us. The red conqueror slept at my side, the sensitive right-angled fingers of one lengthy hand pinioning my ankle.

*

I had slept late the next morning. I opened my eyes on the

139

lake of emerald sunrise slashing the turrets of my old Tower.

A lovely scent filled my nostrils. A soft, gooey, eat-me scent – a delicious oozy pallid grub was squirming in the red fingers of my new guard. He was holding it to my face.

I looked up. My eyes met the gaze of the ape. Its eyes were – something. Quizzical? It had emotions, I wearily supposed, very slightly more complicated than the lust for status, the drive to eat, and the urge to kill.

I wouldn't show again that I even knew that fat grub existed.

The males didn't go to hunt today. There was enough mastodon left to feed the tribe for a week. Even if maggots appeared in it, they wouldn't mind. Probably be delighted, as we would be by salt or spice.

Now I saw why males had been set to guard me. Only males could sit and laze like this. The females, this fat week, needn't search out grubs and roots. So now they must split bones for marrow, they must soften and chew hides in which to wrap the bald infants for the Cold.

Throughout the day, the red ape would appear beside me with, each time, a more succulent worm looping the loop, a bursting banana, a mammoth kidney, a fragrant mango. And finally a dear little lizard which he skinned fresh before my eyes (it was dead, thank goodness) and showed me all its little jelly arteries.

Yes. Definitely quizzical.

I was longing, *hurting* for food. In fact, I thought I might soon starve myself so efficiently I'd die that way.

The ape had a flash of insight. It sat round in front of me so its bulk hid me from the tribe. Surreptitiously offered me the lizard in one hand, the mango in the other. I looked at it. Under the jut of the low red brows, the deep little eyes were alight. I took the mango. The ape-eyes narrowed, the pupils slits. Had I pleased it, that its bandishments were succeeding and its task in working-order at last? Or had I amused it? Somehow I felt I had amused it, but that was likely my own human misconstruction, and I was falling into the old anthropomorphic trap of believing animals must have human reasons for this or that.

*

At intervals through the day, between eating, lazing, and honouring a sleek superb female by letting her search for lice amongst his red hair, the big male visited me with little delicacies – and hid me from the tribe as I accepted them. I began to feel more with it. I had been dizzy with weakness and nightmare. Now I was more able to sort out my strengths from my pains. I was able to realise now my besetting pain was *thirst*. The sun had beat down these last two eternal days. I don't usually drink much, I can go the whole of a hot day without noticing I haven't needed water. But last night I had been gathering the dew-pearls from the stone parapet and tonguing them from my fingers. Now, the hunger at bay in my body and my mind clearer, I realised I was suffering from thirst most of all.

Presently a shadow blacked out my feet and I knew that again the ape was with me. He offered on his long, long, bare, fine-etched palm a soft fruit. I brushed away the eager flies and ate the fruit.

'Thank you,' I said. The ape watched me with a brief attentiveness whenever I said this, and once when I'd omitted it he'd looked inquiring, as if missing part of a ritual.

'I am so thirsty,' I said. I made my tone plaintive. I opened my throat and gasped to show how dry I was. Before he brought the fruit, I hadn't been able to summon enough saliva even to gasp, except very croakily.

The ape didn't go away. It watched. I thought, Is it like a dog, or a dog as dogs were in the wild state before man met and domesticated dogs? Does the ape like being talked to, even if it doesn't know talking has any meaning?

I tried to think of a sign for drinking. I cupped my hands and poured imaginary water down my throat, with some imaginary spluttering and swallowing.

There was no reaction. Well, what did I expect? I thought irritably. A bottle of wine brought?

141

But still the ape squatted, watching me. Perhaps it thought I was putting on a show for its benefit.

'If only you'd let me near that stream down there,' I said.

I stood up. The ape stood swiftly, as if expecting me to make a godlike jump for it. I pointed at the stream. 'Shu-shashusha,' I tried to sound watery and ripply.

Suddenly the ape went down on its hunkers like a big red toad. It thrust its head below its hulking shoulders and urged its flat, receding jaw to and fro. It gurgled and hissed. It just hadn't understood my first mime for drinking. It drinks like a beast, ready to leap up on prey or away from predators.

'Yes! Yes!' I nodded vigorously. Then realising even that meant nothing, I clapped my hands and tried to look happy and eager.

The ape stood erect. It took my wrist. Its fingers are very powerful, powerful enough to tear almost any substance to pieces within seconds, but I think that for it this was a gentle grip. It led me over to a female clasping young.

The female was swollen, very pregnant. She looked, in fact, due any minute. I thought nothing could be more terrifying even to, or especially to, a mindless brute – living in such a tribe, with no midwife. Even in the gutter of the City, there are drugs. But this little ape mother looked contented, sitting placidly rocking her nursling perched on her burgeoning belly.

The red male lifted one of her breasts. She looked up at us, without protest.

The male waited impatiently at me.

When I didn't react, he bent and set his broad mouth to her nipple. He sucked and straightened with a glad gasp, as if to tell me, This is good.

I approached the female, nervous. But she watched me, placid, and if anything she should have been more nervous. I took the hard long orange teat in my mouth.

The milk came almost at once.

It was rich, and sweet, strong as goat-cheese, fresh like liana honey. By my face, the cuddled baby looked up at me

142

from thoughtless yet wondering eyes, raisin eyes.

I stepped back from her, my thirst quenched. Feeling less hungry, too.

'Thank you,' I said to this female who was waiting for me to fatten up as fodder for her infant and her embryo.

They considered me, the female and the great red male looming over me, from their enigmatic recesses of privacy.

Now on my feet and stronger, I looked and saw that here I was near the place that had opened on to my bedroom.

I walked into it. The ape did not stop me, merely accompanied me.

Carpeted with dust and dirt, and walled by trembling fungus. The bed a huddle of torn mattress – the rugs had all been looted by what generations of apes, of nesting squirrels? Now a family of rats bustled in the shreds. Yet what dreams I had suffered on that mattress – dreams of a vast amorphous terror-ridden wonderful place called The World – which I expected never to see, and which, when I was tumbled out into it, was vaster, and more full of terror, and more wonderful – and unspeakably more amorphous.

I stood looking around. The ape watched me, quiescent. When I walked to the leathern hanging, and lifted it (it was a skeleton curtain, now) and entered what had been my secret passage, it followed me silently.

Here I had hidden from my shrill nurse. Here I had poured my soul through my eyes, reaching with my eyes and my soul the mountains and the bay, under storm and under sun and so terribly near and so eternity-far, that I had expected never to adventure through any other of my body's senses. Beyond those conical threatening infinities of stone, I thought now, lies the Northkingdom and also the Ocean. And Atlan. There, Zerd.

Zerd, if Zerd only would rescue me now. Nothing is impossibility to him if he attempt it. Smahil, down in my Mother's teeming sprawl of City? Smahil thinks I have run, I have got out, because I am afraid to face him and be drawn into his sharp orbit. Smahil will be sulking down

143

there while I am meeting a bizarre fate at the hands of these huge brutes.

I turned. More than before, in this little space, the ape towered over me, a great inescapable *fact*. Bulk, muscle, bone, an animal smell. My doom.

I saw a louse jump in its fur. To relieve my own tension, to test my gathering reflexes, I caught and squidged it between forefinger and thumb.

The ape cuffed me lightly across the side of the head. My ear burning, I noted the cuff as approval. The ape's lips drew back from genial cleaver-teeth.

It was proud of me. For a pet, I was showing intelligence.

*

I don't know how many nights I have spent since that time, tormenting myself, asking *how, why* it happened? My mind always returns to one little incident, which I think sums up the *how* of Ung-g the red ape. I see the little bird alighting on the parapet. It's a humming-bird, and at first it is just a supersonic invisibility. A whir, a blur. Its wings clarify as they slow, and it perches on the stone and begins to preen its jewel of a breast with a beak like a darning-needle. It is tiny. It's the size of a big insect, and its wings are gradated violet to blue-tinted cream, and its tail is a trembling dart the violence of turquoise, and silver trembling wattles catch the sun on its tiny head. You can see the stone through its little rosy feet, transparent as rose petals. An ape calf lumbers up to crush it in one articulated fist. Turning from the big superb sleek-muscled female he has been sampling behind her bull's back, the red ape they call Ung-g, and who guards me, knocks the child aside and takes the bird, too terrified to whir away, in his own huge long fist where it trembles and he strokes it and strokes it and begins to croon to it and then opens his fist and, incredulous, the hummer teeters to its wings and then turns into a blur and hums away. The ape child is sprawling in the dust, one of its tusks loose, the ape wife is sprawled as she was left and her master turns to eye her with suspicion and bellows and beats her a great ringing blow for

144

good measure, but the bird is away, singing its heart out (with its ecstatic little wings, no voice) in the purple orchids.

I think that was the *how* of what later happened to Ung-g and I. But the *why* I shall never know till one day my God may show me.

*

As the next days uncoiled their dry dusty lengths, I became familiar enough with the grunts and all the other hideous sounds about me to know that the apes called each other by distinguishing grunts, and they grunted Ung-g at the one watching me. But you couldn't call it a language. It was all expression – screams of offence-taken, bellows of rage, grunts of greed, gurgles of sex-urge, or the low wail of an ape rocking back and forth in the agony of his doctorless pains – the sores like ponds that they have no salves for, the wounds they cannot heal.

*

On the hottest day, they came to kill me.

The mastodon was finished, putrefying below the walls in a zithering swarm of flies. I hadn't known there were so many flies in the entire forest as now pullulated above the remains in the pit down there.

The hunters had not gone out. The lazy life had spoiled them. The females came to them, gnashing their teeth with nothing to bite on, holding their complaining children's empty little hirsute bellies. The males pointed at me. And they all came towards me.

Time had swung. Fate, I thought, resigned, as the apes once more advanced to rend me, as on the day when the little sisters brought me to the Tower. The strong sun spun overhead and sparks danced in and out of my eyes. Their grunts, their heavy flat footfalls coming to me on the stone, even the rasp of their fingers flexing for the action ahead, merged and choked my ears.

And beside me the red ape stood too.

He will be first, he is nearest, I thought.

145

He faced them: he let out a long, lung-searing roar. It was a challenge. It bounced off the hot hills.

The other apes slowed, but did not stop. They were puzzled. Stand aside, join us, said their big loose puzzled gestures.

The ape called Ung-g bent and picked up the great jagged meat-fringed shoulder-blade at his feet.

Hardly believing, they understood. And even more slowly than they, I understood. He was telling them not to hurt me.

They shambled.

He stood, as nearly erect as these creatures on their bent knees with their thrusting heavy shoulders can stand. He hefted the jagged bone. He was daring them. He was protecting me.

They can't rush anything, not even their prey when they're out hunting (except for very small scampery creatures) until they have worked themselves up first. If you stand and face them, and look them in the tiny eye, they can't rush you straight off. It's psychological, I suppose, poor dim dangerous ghastly creatures. A couple of the males stood upright and started a beat session on their chests. Ung-g growled and beat his chest. This worried the entire tribe. They shuffled and some of the females dropped back on all fours and went off to crack marrow-bones.

Ung-g had worked himself up as much as they now. Or better, for he was more purposeful, he had a challenge to back up. This status thing again, man's earliest instinct after that old intrinsic self-preservation.

A bull rushed us. Ung-g's bone-stab met him. The jagged points of the cancerous white bone slurped and drank blood.

The bull lay on the old stone. It was not dying. It bled a lot, and presently would lose consciousness, but none would molest it. They were deeply shocked by Ung-g's action. And suddenly, after a white hot pause, they all howled and rushed on us.

Ung-g seized me and leaped over the parapet.

On a broad bough we turned and regarded them. The

146

tribe did not follow. They hung and gibbered over the parapet, shaking their fists at us, throwing soft fruit.

Ung-g did not look at me after he set me down. He peeled and ate two bananas, slowly. He caught flies and crushed them. He let an hour fade the sun. He got up and started back to the Tower.

Bulls and females started up on the parapet. They screamed at him. They were furious, grinding their teeth, audible even here. They wouldn't let him return. They wouldn't chase him. He was not criminal. But he was outcast. At least temporarily, they would mob and lynch him if he returned to the society whose basic rules he had unforgivably thrown out of line.

Ung-g grunted and glared murderously at me. Daring your peers to harm a pet is one thing. But to be cast out in the cold or (in this case) the sultry jungle night, on account of the pet is quite off-putting.

*

'I'm off home. I won't thank you. You wouldn't understand if I did.'

I started towards the canyon that leads to the hills around the City.

A heavy odorous weight pinned me to the moss. The white grooves of the ape's teeth were inch-fractions from my throat. Only when I had stiffened to the meek immobility of a corpse did the ape roll off me. Now it squatted a yard from me, as though it couldn't care for my proximity. But the corners of its eyes were grim. I was to make no moves of my own.

What had I become now that the tribe had ejected him because of his stand over me? He hated me. I was the cause of his casting-out. Only he must have power to move me.

I could tell, in the following days, how repellent he found me. How soft, how hairless, how tuskless. He threw fruit at me when he hunted meat for himself. He no longer cared to tempt my appetite. We slept in the crotches of twin trees, no double-tree-ing for us – but if I woke in the night and started stealthily to move, Ung-g's instant-waked low growl

147

would thrum from the close darkness, all implacable threat.

Why did he not let me go? I was the symbol of his de-fiance. For me, he had this time to endure till the tribe for-gave or forgot. But for my presence, he would be merely *outcast*. With me there, I symbolised how he had chosen and dared. I was proof, and hated.

We must always sleep at least 125 feet above ground. Otherwise we were not safe from the big cats, climbing like climbing shadows. Nor from the reaching claws or jaws of the saurians that galumphed through the junglethick. Up here, we were able to feel the heat of the sunrise. Yet we couldn't go so high that we were clear to the light. If we ventured out of the subaqueous green gloom that was my daily prison, we might be seen by a condor or winged lizard, and be taloned for prey – as, one morning, we saw a slow patient sloth with lichen growing amongst its fur as its only camouflage or protection, clinging stubbornly to a high branch as a pterodactyl with a ten-foot wing-spread tore it limb by limb from its bourne.

That night there was a snake in the place I lay to sleep in.

It was not a wide snake, but long and voracious. It closed around me instantly. There were orange and purple suckers on the underside of its body, and it fastened them to me as it wound. It was as long as I and wound swiftly.

'Ung-g!' Wildly I approximated the sound I had heard the apes use for the ape I was with. For all I knew, Ung-g meant 'Let us eat' or even 'Curse-ape'.

Ung-g swung to my side. He had caught up the jagged bone with which he had defied the tribe. As he circled me, his hand with the stone in it watchful, I saw that his little eyes, above and below his utter calmness, were wondering at the swiftness of the snake.

There was no place to strike without striking me. Need that trouble him?

I twisted sideways.

The bone shore upon all the snake's coils that side of my body. The bone's points drank and slurped. The snake was broken.

The snake, dying, threshing, squeezed breath from me.

One of its struggles, its scales clashing, lashed Ung-g's ankle.

Ung-g put down the bone. He looked at me. The snake was dead. I was still alive. I was alive only because I had twisted. Had it at last occurred to Ung-g that, though I must remain his, he could rid himself of what he owned by destroying it, though he could not allow it to leave him voluntarily?

Once this had occurred to him, he might stab or strangle me at any time.

I went to the stream to wash the great bone. But it would always be red now.

When I returned, Ung-g's foot still bled. He was examining the bleeding. The wound might or might not have troubled him, his expressions, if he had any, were unreadable by me. But obviously the continued blood troubled him.

I crouched beside him. My hands were still wet from the stream. When I first laid my hand on his wound, he snarled. But I persisted, making no sudden movements, and closed the deep ragged cut a little with the cool pressure of my hand.

I ripped a strip of linen from the hem of my shift. Ung-g growled. He was interested. Perhaps he had always thought my shift a natural part of me, and now thought I had torn a part of myself as a snake sloughs its skin.

I bound the strip into a bandage around the wound. Presently the linen was dark. Ung-g fingered it cautiously, with distaste. But he left it.

Around us, howler monkeys began a curdling chorus. Yet no red had touched the trees to say there was a sun up there, somewhere, setting. Insects began in streams to disturb the forest floor and lower terraces. After them, but not pursuing them, came the ant-eaters and the armadillos scurrying. Next loped jaguar and lynx. Ung-g scooped me up. We fled as high as we dared, till the boughs hooped like elastic under us. And here through the jungle came the seesawing laugh that the jungle dreads.

Crashing saplings, lianas, everything in its path, clawing

149

small monkeys and possum from the foliage, came the ogre from the steaming swamp – the insatiable tyrannosaurus-rex, most vicious creature ever created.

As I looked in the direction of the crashes and screaming foliage, I saw first the foot and knee of the ogre. It stepped daintily, like a gargantuan bird on tiptoe. Much higher, and it seemed off in a different direction altogether, I saw next a little grabbing arm, only the size of the monstrous knee, and curled up against the shining folds of reptilian chest. Then, right beside us, appeared the head. From the hideous mouth, like grass from the snout of a chewing cow, protruded the frantic gesticulating little monkeys and rodents and marmosets which a moment before had been twittering with pleasure as they sun-basked on their boughs.

The tyrannosaurus' eye fixed us.

The pupil was a six-foot slit of black light. It was a slit, a chasm leading into nothing. An abyss of mindless greed lay behind that eye. But it was on us it fixed.

With an instinct strong as a reflex, I willed myself invisible. But I had none of that necessary old psychic power which was born in our ancestors. I cowered, the pit of hell yawning at me – not the bleeding crunching mouth high and huge as a canyon, but the eye – the ruminative eye of the ogre.

An arm came round me. My head was turned from the sight. My gaze was buried in a luxuriance of red fur.

We waited for the cage of claws to come up and grab us. I felt the flex against me of Ung-g's mighty muscles, so tiny to the creature pausing by our towering tree.

Ung-g's hand lifted the great bone.

What doomed attempt he might have made before one of the hands crushed us up, I never knew. A second laugh ululated over the trees. I looked. The eye left us. The head turned.

'It's another one!' I breathed. Together, the ape and I watched the jungle swimming a little under the crackling dance-step as a new brute, a replica of the first, came up behind it.

The new one was smaller. It had no crest. The folds of its

face shone as a million tiny scales reflected the cowering rainbow world.

I'd read my books now damp dust and rat-nests in the Tower library. I had immediate hopes that there would now follow the classic battle for mastery between the two monsters – killing each other neatly in the process. The ape, in spite of being illiterate, seemed to know my hope. It looked at me and blinked. The gesture was a negation, a deliberate hooding of the insolent alien gaze, an equivalent of a head-shake.

One is the other's young, I now thought.

They will merely help each other.

But the smaller, crestless one was a different colour. And formed in a similar proportion to the greater.

One is female, I amended, as the bottomless pit turned on her.

And a rapport, an electric glee, passed between myself and my companion as we realised that after all the two would now engage one with the other.

The female snapped tusks each like a mastodon tusk. But it was a preliminary, maybe even love-play, though it clashed and echoed like iron in a chasm. The male's robot claws came up together, and fastened on her neck-wattles.

He swung her round. She resisted no more. How could she resist this supremest of all males, this glittering metallic reptilian terror? He was behind her, this we could see between the intervening fronds of wood. Now he had clasped her. He was moving, jerking in giant irregular spasms, the slit eyes immobilised without a change of anti-expression, the mouth opened in a rictus that let loose the chewed pulped victims in a drizzle of mangled limbs, of blood and saliva. She stood still, her smaller head motion-less, her little ready hands hanging cuddled up against her breast. Ung-g was tugging me away, away, and I following him too fast for my fear of the unfamiliar boughs, but like a galaxy the protagonists were so vast that wherever we moved we saw them fixed on the jagged horizon. A salty reek pervaded the air, conquered the jungle scents. The male was nearing his paroxysm. He juddered. A parrot flew nearly into his eye, a brilliant scratch on the glazed pupil, as though the slit were a beckoning void of night. The tyrannosaurus was becoming limp. He folded on the female, whose back now supported him. Leisurely, she turned and began to devour him, tearing with those magnificent teeth chunks from the side of his face, drawing his limp body up as more and more of it disappeared fragmentarily into her jaws, while the rest lay still twitching and feebly resisting to the end.

At last all that remained of him was mashed.

She turned her great mindless head over us all.

But she was sated. She lolloped with a matriarchal tread to the swamp. The red sun sank. Howlers dared a roaring chorus.

*

Ung-g picked at his bandage. He meant me to notice the picking. I came and unwound it, motioned him to lick his wound, now cleanly healing in spite of the venom-edged strength of the suckers that had slashed him, and re-wound the linen strip.

I noticed that we had approached language. He told me, by his fingering the linen, what he wanted of my tacitly-admitted skill. And this had come from the tyrannosaurus-siege in the trees. When the second reptile appeared, and was smaller, the expectation and negation had flashed between us as words might have.

'Here's another!' I had exclaimed. And Ung-g had known what I said.

*

When night fell, the darkness suggested such sounds and movements to me, I set about making fire. I knew enough to gather dry plant-life. That's harder to find than I expected. The lower forest is humid, and moist. That's why fungoids are all over the place. I got two dry twigs (after mistaking a stick-insect for one) and sat sawing them together.

The ape, in the neighbouring tree crotch, hardly glanced

152

at me. He had pulled off the bandage. But quite suddenly sparks spat off my sticks, and shot away like tree-hoppers. The ape looked up, so alarmed it forgot to growl.

I was more surprised than it was. I'm not used to being efficient. I hadn't really expected success – just thought Ho, *fire* would be a good idea – and like a game of let's-pretend, anything-to-fill-in-time, I'd set about it.

I sawed more rapidly. And presently a great rose of flame blossomed, and both sticks were alive and alight in my hands.

I dropped them in a shudder. And down there between the roots, I saw them smouldering on the massed leaves of the forest floor.

Two fears beset me – that they'd burn out in the moist down there – or that they'd landed on dry leaves, and terribly would start a full-scale forest fire.

I swung down, grazing my shins.

I flung leaves and foliage on the little busy embers, that ran red amongst them. I siezed a stick and dug a trough of earth around my fire, that it couldn't leap over. I watched in an artist's excitement as the flames reared. I noticed the ape had followed me down.

It approached the fire, not believing it mine nor in my control. It retreated at the thin trough – the heat already was intense. I piled more fuel. 'Huah,' the ape said.

'But you had fire in the well of my Tower,' I said.

The ape stood regarding me, listening to my speech, a great heraldic beast all gold and red in the blaze.

'I suppose your forefathers took the original brand to feed your well from the eruption of an old volcano,' I said. 'You kept it going but couldn't create it. To you fire is a natural phenomenon, unmakeable as sun or storm. Well. Am I a phenomenon?'

I sat down and made signs. I pointed to Ung-g. I put my hands under my head and shut my eyes. Ung-g sleeping. Myself, I sat theatrically upright, watching the fire, tending it, making sure no gaps appeared in it. Then I slept, and while I slept I was Ung-g tending our fire.

This sign-language was an awful step back after the true

speech of the tyrannosaurus' shadow. Then, I had spoken, and instantly Ung-g had answered.

Now, I again pointed to show Ung-g to sleep first.

Ung-g moved to me. I did not reach even his shoulder. Looking right ahead, willing myself still in the proximity of the brute, I could see the nipples spaced like rusty coins on the cavernous chest under the heraldic amber fur. Gently, moving very slowly so as not to disturb or alert me, he took my hands and placed them together in the prayer position I had used to indicate sleep. He put my head on them and with the touch of a feather his long simply-whorled finger-tip closed each eyelid. I was to sleep first.

When I woke, the sickle-curved and star-dot eyes of rodents, reptiles and predators kept at bay appeared and blinked and retreated in phantom rings around the fire, keeping rhythm with the vanishing sparks. Ung-g sat, a branch ready to feed our protector if it waned, a huge bulk of radiant energy – both fire and ape.

\*

The next day Ung-g left me. I was alone. I was afraid. I had wanted to be alone, so that I could pick my way back to civilisation. Now I no longer knew in which direction the City lay, in which directions the jungles thickened into light-years of impassable savagery.

Had Ung-g left me because I was a witch? I had made fire. No longer was I a possession of the ape's.

I cowered beside my flames, watching frantically to see they didn't die.

Darkness. No Ung-g. I hoped for him at every rustle. I didn't mean to sleep.

\*

When I woke, still in teeming darkness, the embers low, I knew a close presence. Cautiously I opened one eye, a fraction at a time, having divined by instinct which eye was nearest the instinctively-felt presence. Looking down at me, watching each of my fractional cares, was the ape – quizzical.

'Ung-g!' I said.

And he understood that welcome.

This huge creature, which at one time I had looked on as an unpredictably loyal dog, and which at one time had looked on me as a pet with faint beginnings of intelligence, now squatted itself on its haunches beside me. It looked away from me, and then glanced at me, pretending not to. This was leading behaviour. What was up? What differences could I note? A tightness on my throat. As I moved, I felt a little bang against my breast.

Aghast, I stared down at myself – two gleaming diamond eyes stared back up at me.

'Ung-g! Another snake!'

Ung-g chuckled.

But it wasn't a snake. It lay, looped about my neck, graceful, moveless, a serpent of twisted gold in exquisite coils. About its inset eyes, standing out from them in the air a half-inch either side of them, stood the little blue rainbow diamonds in dark engender.

'Ung-g!' I said stupidly (feeling always that doubt – was the sound a name at all?). I touched the snake. It was icy cold and beautifully wrought. A binding-magic? A taboo-brand? Ung-g watched me, expressionless so far as I could tell, but most intent.

'A present?' I had almost forgotten the word.

I didn't know how to show delight it would understand, or even recognise. I smiled. And found my eyes were ready to shed tears. The wait without Ung-g had demoralised me.

I stroked and stroked my miracle necklace. 'It is rare and marvellous,' I said. 'Where in the old Gods' names did you find it? People – are there people near from whom you took this?'

Ung-g took me to the place. Our journey lasted nearly a day.

'This reminds me of Atlan,' I said as the forest grew more and more tremendous, opening endlessly out in vista after vista. The trees were giving way to smaller scrub, rich with flowers and other flowers which were really clans of insects, which after you'd disturbed them circled frantically about in mazy patterns very like the snowflakes I saw magnified in the Atlan laboratory, then settled back on their twig in a sneaky camouflage, the head fly folding its wings like the foremost pink-petals, the other insects all in their places, the smallest ones with little wings green-veined like end leaves. I was fascinated and kept disturbing these poor little flowers so I could watch them shoot up in disorder, circle in a big snowflake and then become a flower again. Soon Ung-g noted my interest and he went out of his way to lead me past the 'flowers' and started bothering them himself, standing back to watch me watching them. We began climbing and sliding. The scrub clothed the sides of innumerable steep conical hills which weren't too bad to climb, in spite of their gradient, because of all the tussocks of vegetation and foot-holds and hand-holds – little yawning holes in which you could sometimes see a pair of inquisitive eyes or the warning hiss of gleaming patterned scales. At first I'd been scared they might be termite hills.

My shift was dark with sweat when the hills slowed and steadied. I could feel my heart pumping. We stood on the westerly slope of a cone we'd just negotiated. Almost directly overhead, the sun pulsed in a maelstrom of glitter.

The rocks about us glittered, specked with mica, answering the sun. The sun was so fierce it could have dried that fire we'd stamped to death.

Ahead of us lay a plain of scrub, fallen tree-trunks dried in their rot, rocks I could already feel blistering my feet.

We did not siesta. The ape was a specialised hunting animal. I wondered how it could manage in that lush fur, then wondered if perhaps all the strands were creating infinitesimal private breezes.

The rocks hurt less than I expected. They were light and full of holes, like creamy charcoal, holding air and cushioning the pain.

And we entered, by afternoon, the turquoise bar of verdure which had beckoned on the horizon.

White waterfalls shot down like comets.

'Is it the waterfalls causing this disturbance of faint light all within the shade?' I asked.

The ape was used by now to my speechifying. He tolerated it. Perhaps he thought it was a nervous tic of mine, or a pathetic attempt at camouflage far less skilful than the flower-insects'. Did he connect my speech with his tribe's speech? In comparison, mine was quite bird-like, more complex and rippling than ape-grunts, ape-grunts, ape-grunts.

'*Oh.*' I was enchanted. 'They are butterflies, Ung-g.'

And wherever we trod the dark velvet fragrant moss, we roused vaporous columns, flickering pillars of wings – jady butterflies who sparked like humming-birds at the turn of an antenna, splotched things like flying orchids, and drifts of white like a snowfall settling back once more on the moss.

'Oog,' Ung-g uttered.

My feet had splashed, instead of moss, water. We were in a glade. It was very quiet.

I couldn't believe my eyes. I knelt in the deathly cold water. I touched it, yet hardly daring, pulling my hand back at once. Yes, a great hoard, shining and beckoning more below than above the wide asymetrically spread pool. Ropes of pearls thick enough for a mountaineer. Emeralds blazing like drowned puma's eyes. The petrified violets of amethyst, caverned in settings half time's age, made from –

'Ung-g! This metal is orialc! I've never seen it outside of the secret Continent! It must have been drowned here before the sealing.'

I lifted an immaculate necklace. It broke, the silk strand rotted, and rubies rolled and ran and burned.

And now, about the jewels, I saw the bones in the water. And one socketed skull staring up at me was not there at all, but a livid reflection, and when I lifted my eyes there it hung staring at me from a branch over the pool. And on all the branches hung old chains and human bones.

'You got my snake here?' I said.

Its gold-wire tongue flickered in its cold jaws.

'It is probably laid in a deep curse aeons old.'

Its chill struck in. But I couldn't take it off and fling it from me with the ape watching.

157

To the ape these were only bright pebbles. But it moved quietly. If I had been anthropomorphist, I should seriously have been tempted to say 'reverently'.

'There are no crowns here. Nothing to tell me to whom these bones, this hoard, belonged – or belong – nor who laid them here.'

The ape rose when I rose. But a horror had seized me of advancing farther into the vaporous darkness with all the swirling wings a-tremble ready to shroud us.

'We must go back,' I said. 'This is a demon's place. This is part of the jungle's old insanity. Already it is wrapping us round.'

As soon as I saw the bright mica of the plain I ran for it. There was a burst of new birdsong, and songs of little things rubbing together legs and wing-cases. But, alas the sun was no longer fierce and was the more terrible for that. 'Don't let's be left here at night,' I pleaded Ung-g.

*

We crouched amongst the cone hills. Cobalt shadows seeped across the rock. We were safer from predators here than ever in the jungle. And farthest, too, from the stretches of the swamps where the mists writhe and the fevers rise and the saurians drag their alien bulks from the ooze. Yet why was the air still so chill? The shrub on the turret above us waved vague fingers on the chill airs.

Suddenly the whole landscape shivered. A crack, a blindness, and the turret of the hill above us had been shorn from its allotted place and tumbled downslope in a bumping grinding disintegration.

'That was lightning!' I shouted.

The sky tightened itself into a bruised blood-orange. The trees across the plain, brooding over the hoard and the pool, shimmered like heat-haze. 'We'll be struck,' I moaned as again the lightning whipped.

It suddenly rained torrents. Within minutes the gully where we crouched had become a rushing flood carrying with it sticks and stones.

The sticks were small boughs by the time we'd scrambled

up the glutinous slope. Ung-g seized my wrist. He dragged me, quite literally. As the rain slashed and stang, I closed or half-closed my eyes. I couldn't see where we were going, in what direction we were going. The ground kept altering under my feet. Now I was dragged stumbling up a stinging scree, now we were falling in a slither of mud and gravel and squeaking creatures washed from their safe holes.

When Ung-g dragged me under the waterfall, it made very little difference to the sound and the pouring. But then the drumming of the water came from *outside*. We were *enclosed*.

I opened my eyes and unstuck my lashes. We were in a cave.

Rough earth and rock walls. A low and lowering ceiling, with drips in it, falling to whirl away in little channels and grooves. Ung-g pulled me down hunkering beside him. Together we stared out at the colourless sheet of the water-fall screening the cave entrance, and to either side through that the exactly similarly torrential storm drenching the green forest so mercilessly that the hail bounced again high into itself from the soaking leaves.

I looked about me nervously.

Had Ung-g not checked that this was an uninhabited cave? It seemed to go a long way back into impenetrable murk, the roof sloping lower as it went. Nasty thoughts of cavebears.

At every rumble I started and looked with straining eyes behind us whirling hallucinations starting up in the gloom. But only the thunder growled, only the lightning screamed.

Ung-g glanced aside at me, irritated by my nerviness. He reached out a big paw and stilled me.

My shift was plastered to me. It was sticky with weather. I realised the continuous renewal of the rain had warmed me. Now that the moist fabric was being left to dry, it clung like an octopus with pneumonia.

I sneezed convulsively, and again.

Ung-g pulled me against him. He grasped me in against his mighty ape chest. I snuggled, the warmth crept from

159

his fur, in which I twined my fingers and so fell asleep lullabyed by the storm.

*

I wondered where I was. And, knowing, I wondered who and how was the ape. Still it held me, holding itself stiff and watchful so it should not disturb me, primal man-life overcoming its revulsion at the debased tuskless thing I had become.

I looked up. The brow-ridges lowered to me, and the little amber eyes deep under those.

'The sun is shining out there,' I said in the exaggerated sunny voice I needed to make myself understood. I waved a hand at the big light outside.

A deep odd smile passed and deepened between us. It was a lovely smile, warm and sudden and more relaxing than all my dreams had been. My toes tingled. I felt tremendous well-being and safety.

Ung-g turned me in his arm, against his chest, settling me cherishingly. He stretched. When he yawned, his gums and the disappearing convolutions of his throat were a healthy rose pink and the sun struck gloss off his teeth and tusks.

The waterfall curved in a frantically motionless arc of iridescent shimmer across our cave entrance. We paused at its fringe of sparkling wet orchids, then ducked our heads and raced into and through it, Ung-g grabbing my hand.

I spluttered. I hadn't held my breath.

Ung-g looked at me and gave that low chuckle. I wish now I could describe that chuckle. I can't even hear it properly in my mind's ear. I know no human could ever have made it. It was too deep, too free, a fresh-minted *new* sound at the very root of humour.

Not-quite-man had learnt to laugh. It made the cackles and trills of our own laughter, in fact all the details of civilised man, sound weak and empty.

When we hunted for fruit we made the forest laugh too. We pulled whole wanton boughs of rich gourds dribbling purple beads of juice down on ourselves. And after all it wasn't wanton – immediately whole troops of excited monkeys, and flights of honking toucans, made us into a procession, and squabbled after us for fruit and seeds. Getting out of the way of two green monkeys swinging at each other with gnashing teeth from neighbouring branches, a ripe berry the size of a pumpkin changing hands and disintegrating a little more at each scolding swing. I pulled down a tangle of liana which at once wrapped itself round me with the celerity of a nest of electric eels. Ung-g watched me in utter disbelief and eventually disentangled me while the monkeys, munching, hung to watch.

And I was left still tangled in the last steely spirals and tendrils. Ung-g's hackles rose. He stared at something at the end of the glade.

I writhed out of the coils. There, just entered the glade, stood a massive greying ape. And another, and another. The hunters of the tribe.

*

The tribe were discomposed. Perhaps they had never expected it this way. They were meeting their outlaw on his ground, instead of theirs. This territory thing, from which springs most of their confidence and rules of 'right' and 'wrong', now sapped them of their aggression.

Ung-g merely stood and let a growl drool from his throat.

The leading ape moved forward. In their hands the apes held clubs and stones and antlers with scarlet tips.

Ung-g's leisurely almost casual growl gathered volume. There could be no friendliness between creatures who had last parted in mutual threat. The only solution was for the other apes to turn aside. Ung-g could not turn aside in his wilderness.

But the apes were many. And Ung-g was a pariah. Their instinct was to hunt and destroy the creature different from the herd. They would not turn aside either.

They came, their leg-joints stiff with deliberation.

Their luck hunting had been ill. One dead iguana hung over one brute's shoulder. They looked at me. They looked at Ung-g. Ung-g could redeem himself.

The leader pointed at me. All together, guttural like rocks speaking, they gave tongue.

Ung-g blinked a slow repulsive No, showing the oyster-colour whites of his eyes.

Working himself up in a hurry, the leader ape lumbered forward beating his chest and emitting screams like needles in our ears.

I retreated up a tree and sat among the silent monkeys with their bug-eyed appreciation of violence. This retreat would be no guarantee of hiding once my would-be kidnappers had done their work below, but now at least I could stay out of the way. It would be massacre, I knew. My affection for the red animal called Ung-g swelled through my fever of pity for myself recaptured.

Simultaneously, and from opposite sides, two apes leapt like oversize squirrels and landed gouging and slavering on Ung-g. Ung-g stayed upright, I didn't know how. His huge muscles shone bulging as he tore grip after grip from his throat, again and again to be savagely replaced.

Roll on the ground, Ung-g, I thought. Then I knew why he was straining his toes and balance, why he was still upright. Once he was down, the pack would be on him.

The other apes circled, waiting for an opening where they could rush in for their share without hurting their two comrades.

The glade began to gurgle. Everywhere came these ghastly sounds of beasts waiting to kill, beasts that were nearly man and to whom killing was gloating.

Then I was up on my branch beside myself. *'Ung-g!'* I yelled, *'Ung-g!'* The red monster looked up and heard me and lifted in greeting the red antler it had torn from the grasp of the dying ape and swung round with it and shore into the fleshy abdomen of the other attacker. This backed, thick slow blood between its fingers, holding its life in to itself. The other apes were reluctant this time to spring in. One of Ung-g's attackers with his throat lying beside him on the turf, the other gripping his life-blood as one grips hour-glass sand, and Ung-g at bay in possession of the antler. And the antler waiting.

162

Three apes sprang this time, again simultaneously. Now I closed my eyes. The frightful sounds made me open them again. Ung-g was stabbing. An ape fell back with a red hole in his head. A watching ape hurled a stone, a piece of fallen comet. The stone met another attacker squarely in the back, and he whirled with a shriek and beat the mistaken one senseless with a couple of blows. Ung-g had shorn his way now through his immediate attackers. He was making for the leader, the king ape, a monument of greying crimson snarling over seven feet high.

The leader waddled mightily forward, his arms open twitching ready to grapple and hug Ung-g to him.

Ung-g too was walking forward, rolling from side to side like a heavyweight wrestler watching for an opening. His head was down and his arms out. Then suddenly he put both feet together and leaped. Ung-g's weight caught the king full in the chest and he staggered back, wheezing. At that instant Ung-g's antler ripped down followed by the agile tusks. Quite casually, Ung-g's hand ripped the ear from the side of the king's head. But the throat was the target. Bellowing his eternal disapproval of what had happened, the king fell. The leaves spun.

The tribe now pulled together, and stood swaying shoulder against shoulder. Their leader was dead. Down there, inert, the life and power and kingdom gone out of him. The fight had gone out of them.

Ung-g must have been reeling from his wounds. But he stood impassive waiting for them to shuffle out of the clearing.

I was already down the tree and halfway across the turf to him. I caught him.

'Ung-g,' I said, and repeated it again and again, the only word I knew he knew, putting into it all my gratitude and marvelling. 'Now you can return to them. Now you can go any time and return, and be their king and take their king's harem and all his rights and his glory.'

Ung-g was not mutilated, merely gashed here and there. I ran to the stream and brought back water cupped in my hands. He would not let me do too much to him. His eyes

163

were blazing. His fur was electric with victory. He grasped me – but with the most extreme gentleness – and pointed to a huge cup-blossomed flower dangling just before us. He drew his finger in a long line down into the heart of the flower, and then out again, still in the same shaft. At first I couldn't begin to grasp what this meant, till I saw his finger had followed a sunbeam piercing the flower to its centre. Ung-g then made the most unequivocal gesture, drawing the same line from himself to the front of my shift. He would pierce me, but as the sunbeam pierced the flower. Looking steadfastly and questioningly in my face, he raised my tattered shift.

Butterflies whirled in the pillar of sunlight that rose where only yesterday there had been a giant tree, now crashed full length by the night's storm. A young bamboo was fully a foot taller than yesterday.

The green monkeys, recovered from their fright at violence, now pelted us with nuts and flowers. The nuts were rather hard, but the flowers rained down like a bridal rain. I laughed up into Ung-g's face.

I had expected him to hurt me in spite of himself. But he had thought how to move, how to be patient, how to be gradual. He was urgent yet tender. Plenty of men have raped me. It has taken primaeval man, an animal of the forests, to show me how tender tenderness can be.

*

I knew that now Ung-g stayed in the jungle for me. He had no dream of leaving me. I gave him all I could. I knew some doom hung over us. But I would say to myself, *Why shouldn't this last? We have no common speech, but he has a strength to keep me safe in this dangerous paradise, and a tenderness matching, that no man can give me whose speech is mine.*

He would grow morose and sullen, I knew, as apes do.

But before that one or the other of us must have been destroyed by our paradise.

Meanwhile, he has shown me a wonder that passes my

164

understanding. This demon of the wild has sacrificed himself for me, and loves me for it.

I am his pet, his possession, but he is passionate about it, and gentle. Perhaps it can't be called love. Perhaps it is having fought for me that has given me this importance for him. But understanding has grown with us. Perhaps it can be called love.

Of course I have thought since those days, and those thoughts, that my idea that now he could return and take up the leadership of his tribe was wrong. Perhaps by killing the king he was more than ever outlaw.

But I do know he loved me. We lived it. He swung me off my feet and carried me over streams I could have waded – then flung me to the filigreed moss and did not always take me, but let me worry the palms of his naked hands with a feather, and chuckled if I attempted to wrestle with his great strength. We bit the fruit from each other's mouths.

In the City ways, I had seen diseased men, and men whose avarice or brutality or humourless pomposity was a disease – and I had thanked my God many times a day, till Rubila's memory faded, that I was not forced to lie with men.

Now in this clean fierce hot green gloom I offered my Cousin praise that in a sidelong dimension he is my guardian. I thought in pain of the little tart Aka tarting herself into her mental grave by the Canal. I imagined marvellous forays Ung-g and I could make one day into the City to rescue the poor hopeless child. Sometimes I blessed my little Seka, and thought how lucky she was to have lost me when she was still too little to care, and how she would grow up in the rustling house on stilts, and have adventures like pouring hot water on the ants in the scullery, or spitting in the well of enemy children. No more disorganised mother dragging her round the known world in dangerous hare-brained adventures.

Then, as Ung-g taught me to lose my fears and swing lither through the odorous branches, I knew a bruise had lifted off my heart.

The bruise had lain so long, so deep and heavy, half I had forgotten what it meant. Then I searched back. And I knew the bruise had been my husband Zerd, and that though I remembered him, at long last my heart had forgotten him.

*

Ung-g lifted his head and his nostrils flared. He scented what? Later I heard the baying of the hunting hounds.

This belling rising musical sound spread like water – like a flood – through the jungle.

Ung-g and I took, naturally, to the trees. But the baying followed. We had been scented. The hunters' hounds had smelt ape-man, which tastes like long pork and is as near as the hunters of the City come to cannibalism.

Presently a brindled hound with pink transparent ears was snuffing up our trunk, its paws placed high, its keen tail a blur. Others joined it, and before the hunters followed and speared or smoked us down, we must get away again.

Slowly, almost in a circle, we were forced towards the canyon that leads to the City.

The jungle became patchy. I had not noticed this in the old days. I noticed it now, after the lush virgin verdure of the inner forest. There were scars where clearings had been axed. There were acres of poisoned soil where men had attempted to bring their agriculture and their chemicals to the forest earth, where the men had failed to gain a foothold for their greed but where the growths had been razed and stunted, where the giant trees that had stood pulsing since the dawn of time had been chopped and felled and would never in this world be again, where secondary growths had sprung up like scrubby weeds.

Still the pink-eared hounds followed in full cry.

Now there were bones and black places where the hunters had smoked trees, or made eating-fires. Ung-g did not like these borders of the forest. His hackles rose and a deep thrumming growl began to reverberate in his throat. The berserk anger of the ape was growing in him.

Suddenly the pack burst from the trees and flew at us.

166

The little trees here were not cover enough. The foliage was scanty and would not hide us at all from the men, the boughs were too light to bear us high enough out of reach.

Ung-g flung me over his shoulder and made a leap dizzy as true flight.

I found that he had landed us, presently, after a half-dozen leaps, beside a large low shape close to the earth and crawling and buzzing. This was a swarm of flies, very happy about the corpse of a great buffalo with several arrows protruding from sticky rivers of blood dried black. Perhaps recently the hunters had shot it and then lost it and it had died days later.

It always makes me feel sick with hatred when I see something big and beautiful and strong like that lying under flies and senselessly – it hadn't even been used for food, just terminated and left, its gallant horns still white in the sun.

But I choked as we came near it. The smell was terrible. Ung-g pulled me round it. There was a great yawn in its stomach, where jackals had discovered it and gnawed through to its intestines. Flies marked the loops of the entrails on the ground, and there was a movement of maggots.

I held my breath and thought I should strangle as Ung-g dragged me through the hole.

Inside the buffalo I thought I knew what hell would be. Dark, slimy, stench. Suffocating one's nostrils, one's throat, and claustrophobic too. A squirm against one's flesh of gorging invisible maggots. But Ung-g was right. If this couldn't throw the dogs off our scent, nothing could.

It was all we could have done. There was no water near to lose the dogs in. But though the dogs cannot possibly have smelt us through the corpse, the buffalo itself attracted them.

Ung-g held me close as we heard the dogs snuffling around outside.

A revulsion took me. The top of my head seemed to be pressing in on me. The hairy muscular arm around me seemed total nightmare. Ung-g was alien, our relationship a hallucination. I nearly screamed – it was not fear of the hunters, of mankind, that kept me silent – and not fear of opening my mouth into the stench: but of the moving maggots against my face.

The only thing that kept me sane was a consciousness of my own nobility. I was suffering this for Ung-g alone. He couldn't know – I could never tell him even if I wanted to – but I had nothing whatsoever to fear from the men. It was only he they would harm.

Then daylight. A dog had thrust its nose through to us. At once the pack had widened the hole. And now the buffalo's belly peeled back. And men were looking down at us.

They were Palace hunters. Once again, Prince Progdin to the rescue.

There was a silence of mutual amazement. Even the dogs stayed still.

Then, scrabbling frantically, the men were hauling me out. Horror was written on their faces. I was amused by this, even in my consternation, in the crumbling of my world. They looked as though they had stood looking down into the brink of the incredible and unspeakable.

'Don't kill him! Don't kill him!' I screamed as they rescued me. I had to change my cries to, 'Don't kill it!' before the spear-men understood me.

'Progdin! Don't let them kill the ape!'

I had never seen the dark Prince so disturbed. 'I have heard of no such kidnapping in all my life,' he said, 'in which the human being has been rescued safe and in one piece. None of us will ever be able to imagine what sufferings you have been through.'

He expected my fervent thanks for turning up so luckily, for setting his quivering dogs in the first place on the ape's trail.

'Don't harm the ape,' I said.

I tried to reach Ung-g. He was noosed and bound in a big net. He was slung over two ponies. The man he first succeeded in killing, in the madness with which he tried to reach me to rescue me from the Men, was carried too for burial.

I was set on a pony and Progdin rode alongside me.

'I want that ape to be given to me, when I reach home,' I said.

'I very much regret, madam, that after all you have been through you will not be reaching home.'

'But you know, Prince, that I am the Dictatress' daughter. I claim now my birthright. At last I shall make myself known to her.'

'These are all my men, and they follow my orders, madam, as to whose birthrights are recognised and whose are not. By my courtesy, you shall indeed be taken to your parent.'

'You can't take me to my father!'

'I am working with your father, madam. He has long waited your coming. You have never met him, I think. This evening that omission will be rectified. He will be very grateful.'

'He'll kill me!'

'I should presume it most likely, madam.' The Prince bowed.

*

Downriver to the High Priest's island. A last look of agony exchanged with my Ung-g, farewell for ever to the marvellous friend who has saved me again and again only to be destroyed by me, by my fate again tangling in on me.

Though the days, all the days, in the forest had been bright and clear, we rode through a yellow mist in the City's evening.

Though the forest floor had been carpeted like the layers and layers of soft resilient expensive carpets in nomad tents, though the foliage had been luxuriant with thick colour and life, the City trees had been pollarded like ogres' clubs, and stood skeletal against the red dying grin of the sun, already a scarlet skull.

Sunset over the river, and we were sculled to the lower shore of the secret pyramid.

Now bound, but allowed to walk upright, I was escorted up the hill. It grew steeper and steeper and I hardly tried to keep upright, hoping I would slide backwards and perish in the sea contaminated by this artificial excrescence, yet without the courage deliberately to fling myself backward.

The chasm at the top of the mountain. Looking down into the rumbling depths.

No Smahil emerging this time to wave swords and slaughter guards.

And the Prince indifferent, it seemed, as to whether I were rescued or tipped in. If Smahil had appeared, I am sure he might have helped him again. But now he gave impassive orders, and suddenly I had been thrown into the abyss.

\*

A moment upside down, on my head in the air so to speak. Waiting for the crack and snap of my neck breaking.

Then I landed. And bounced. And landed again.

Invisible from above, a great net or woven bridge had been slung not far below the lip of the chasm. Into this I fell, and now with a creaking of straining ropes, it was slowly lowered farther and farther into the depths.

The blackness rose to meet me, ever more and more intense, thick and soft as old velvet, ever blacker.

Then the platform, or hammock, or whatever I was crouched helpless on, strained sideways. We seemed to be turning corners and traversing shafts. Steadily a red glow grew from below. It became smoky and airless, yet cold with a shallow empty biteless chill.

Now I saw the vast vaulted chamber into which I was being lowered to pay my last family visit. It stretched away into diaphanous mists. It was shrouded in a gloom that was many-coloured yet, because of its size and chill, seemed of one monochrome tone. Immediately below me gaped a pool which I knew must be the sea – a hatch, in fact, into the ocean which surrounded this monstrous shell. On the galleried sides of the pool stood people. There was a throne stretching up to a spire. On the throne sat a tall pale still figure. My woven platform tumbled me in front of him and I fell properly to my face before him. I had only just missed the pool – a literally bottomless pit, the entrance to the world's waters.

I stood. The platform that had borne me rustled away again up into the vast gloom. I was with my Father.

# PART FIVE

# MY FATHER

'So you are Cija.'

It was a harsh pallid voice, which yet seemed to have no body to it. It seemed not to come from vocal chords, from a throat with saliva and warmth in it, from lungs.

I thought I would never speak to him. I didn't want my voice touching his ears. He had given me such life as I had so far lived. Now let him take my life and be done.

Looking round quite frankly, but without turning my head, I saw the serried ranks of priests about his throne. The faces of fanatics, and of troglodytes, thin bloodless lips, glaring hollow eyes, and pupils and irises faded with the beginnings over them of that gloom that comes to saints and the blind.

Then I saw what shared my Father's twin-seated throne, what lolled there covered with jewels and a long mantle of black sharkskin like the priests' robes, and I stared.

It was an alligator that reclined there, absolutely hung with jewels, dripping gems, its little eyes the only obviously alert eyes in that company, its nostrils dilated on its stretch of snout, its myriad teeth filed each to a point and gilded, its little arms hanging relaxed as the tyrannosaurus' had, the nails gilded and set with baby emeralds, necklaces round its obese throat, its scales polished, its soft pale belly and folded breasts and exposed genitalia cunningly embellished, its tail languid in the sea-pool.

I remembered the whispered stories.

My Father by his vows was celibate. (My mother, Smahil's witch-mother, were secrets even less whispered.) But by divine right he chose and honoured his paramour, which being a female alligator could not be called a breaking of his vows.

The silence stretched on. I would not ask one question.

My Father's lips opened again.

'You are the woman's daughter,' he said.

I immediately broke my own vow of silence. This was too good to let pass in front of these besotted worshippers.

'And yours, Father,' I said.

From the folds of robe on the throne poked like a tortoise-neck a wizened hand, so pale I believed that possibly some miracle had withdrawn the blood from his veins, with nails each about two inches long – grown so long, in fact, so far from their cuticles and roots that they twisted and spiralled a bit at the ends.

The hand shook. The fingers ordered me to silence.

I'll make him blush, blood or not, I swore. 'I am honoured to meet my fate here,' I said. 'I have escaped death in far lands because men knew I was your daughter.'

There was no move from the priestly ranks. But I saw a few of the bloom-shelled eyes slide towards him and each other.

My Father stood up in his chair. The black mantle fell back and there was the long white gown that has gleamed out on so many adoring congregations.

'Silence!' he ordered, his disembodied voice shrill. 'This is blasphemy, for which you will be thrice damned.'

'Then damn me, my Father. I wait the only blessing your soul can give.' I knelt upon the steps, my neck bowed meekly.

'You have been cursed from birth,' came the voice I at last believed. 'You will be sacrificed at the dark of tomorrow's midnight.'

*

At once the steps on which I knelt started floating away from the throne. The throne floated away, punted by a priest, into invisible caverns. The entire floor of this hollow pyramid was sea, not simply one pool as I had thought, and everything on it was a raft.

Now my steps, navigated by a black-wrapped figure, were entering a cave hung with trembling treasure –

fire-flies clinging massed against the rock, which all stirred and winked as we appeared.

In the green glint I could see the floating bed, a big stabilised cradle rocking gently on the deep tide.

'Stay here,' said the navigator, helping me roughly from raft to bed, and punted away again. 'I've no choice,' I said bitterly.

I lay and watched the walls. They were tangled with the roots of the trees outside cracking through the stone of the pyramid slabs. Long blind slow-worms meandered through the mazes. If only I could get word to my Mother. I am here! I am home! Send your soldiers! But I had left it too late. This was what had befallen from my delusions of nobility hours ago when I told myself how I suffered to save Ung-g's love from my kindred, and had instead brought both of us to ruin.

Till tomorrow midnight, then. I would have no way, lying here under the dark stone hours, of knowing when the first midnight arrived, nor how many more exciting last moments were left me to breathe and see and hear and yet not hope.

*

From my floating bed, and at least a day later, I could see into the main chamber. I could see as the rafts and the steps and the throne and my Father and his mistress were again punted to their places for an audience.

In miniature, like a little bright dark dream, I could see the visitors regally lowered in the net.

A slim small man and a somewhat plumper girl. They stepped out and made their obeisances. Smahil and Katisa.

The shock I felt (and I'd thought myself incapable in these last embalmed hours of any more shock ever) I felt in my marrow.

Was all this a deeper plot than I had imagined? Smahil and Katisa – not merely sleeping together – but spying together?

But my Father's first words solved that misapprehension.

174

'I am pleased at last to meet you,' my Father said benevolently.

Did he know what Smahil knew – that Smahil also is his child? This must be Smahil's first meeting too with our Father!

'I am overcome by reverence to find myself before one for whom I have worked faithfully since my return with the Northern regiments,' said Smahil, more tactful than myself.

'Rise, young ones,' oilily said the priest. 'You have done well, little Katisa, to bring this convert here.'

Katisa was his favourite – perhaps he even has his eye on her as a successor to the lazy-lidded alligator? – he treated her quite differently from everyone else and she, in this dread place, was very kittenish.

'How long I have wanted him to meet you, Holy One,' she said after her (conversational) pat-on-the-head. 'We have so much confided in each other our hopes and fears for the realm that should be yours, Holy One. How often he has told me that I am the only woman he can open his heart to.'

I was too far away to watch properly. I wanted to see Smahil's eyes wandering thoughtfully over our Father, summing him up, hating him, yet wondering as I had if there is any of the Father in the child.

I was too far away to see anything of this and probably it just wasn't like that at all. I am never good at interpreting Smahil.

Now our Father began sonorously to praise and re-praise, in the most sincere insincerity, the news Smahil had brought and the tasks he had undertaken and the quality of his loyalty so far proven and the even more highly-coloured quality of his loyalty if in the future proven.

But yes, even my Father knows that worship of him is in itself not sufficient to send men gladly to their deaths – and that men of action do not live by worship alone, though life may be a different matter for priests and alligators.

My Father began presently to add remarks about sub-

175

stantial rewards, about emeralds in a hoard of great price
– 'Or, if you are not an emeralds man, a rather descrimin-
ately hand-picked harem a certain mogul regrets he has no
further possible use for . . . '

Smahil's attention wandered wholly back to the chat. He
finished eating the apple he had drawn from his pocket
during the loyalty business, and flipped the core at the
haughty alligator.

'There is a little matter of a woman,' he said. 'A
woman called Cija – ' he did not even look in the High
Priest's direction for the High Priest's reaction – 'who
quite literally vanished, some few months ago, from a sort
of dinner-party being held in my honour at a house where-
in she was resident on sufferance.'

Both Katisa and the High Priest had their eyes fixed on
him.

'Now that woman had left unsettled a debt she owed
me,' Smahil said, and I could hear how he said it between
his teeth. 'I want nothing so much as to strangle her with
my own two bare hands, for certain ills she has done me in
her own way, and if anyone else has deprived me of that
pleasure I should vow by binding oaths to treat them in
the same way. Can she be found for me?'

Our parent thoughtfully ran his fingernail along his
teeth, like a boy with a stick along a railing fence.

'As it happens,' he said lightly, 'we have just such a
woman here. Can it be, I wonder, that she is the Cija you
want? We need her disposed of. We were going to make a
sacrifice of her by midnight. But my priests are good for
nothing' – he nodded at them and they stared expressionlessly ahead – 'after such orgies. They lose all control and
are useless for days after. Can it be that you would be really
grateful for a chance to – commit – this sacrifice personally?'

'I would prove my gratitude with all the ardency within
my power.' Smahil bowed fervently and clicked his spurs.
His short cloak swirled out and all his medals glittered. He
looked as though plenty of little services would be within
his power.

'Join us here in the hour before midnight,' the priest said and made signs to be paddled away.

'I need first to meet the woman and he assured that she is the one I seek,' Smahil said.

'This you shall do,' the priest decided after due thought. 'It is a reasonable and just request. Tonight, then, at the golden hour.'

The priest drew himself to his full height as the Throne and the raft on which the visitors had stood drew apart in the water. He grew taller and taller. He towered over the alligator, yet his head remained the same size. A gap of space appeared between his feet and the Throne-dias on which he had stood. His feet dangled. He had levitated.

Though he had accomplished this supernatural feat all under his own steam, once the suitably shaken Smahil and Katisa were out of sight he collapsed shivering and sweating from the effort, and, crumpled shaky in his big carved chair beside the obscene lolling beast, he was poled away.

The apple-core Smahil had tossed eddied and circled to my chamber. Taking care not to disturb the priests on guard, I manoeuvred my bed near it. I reached precariously. I held and nibbled the apple core that had been in Smahil's pale mouth.

*

Smahil's eyes narrowed, the left more than the right.

He said, 'This is she.' And all the priests drew aside to let him hate me.

Smahil said in a low voice, his words running together, 'Was that child mine?'

I had to think back before I knew he meant Seka. I said 'No.'

'His?'

'Zerd's, yes.'

'Then you'll have to lose it, Cija,' Smahil almost spat at me. 'I'm extending no roof, no protection, not a morsel of bread, to any spawn of his.'

I had thought of leaving Seka to the household on stilts. 'You're insane,' I said more violently than, in this situation, I had meant. 'You want me to abandon her, you don't know where?'

'Urga's Mother would take her.'

'Can you get me away from here at all, Smahil? It will be awfully dangerous.'

'I have only to bring a force of marauders with me at midnight. But I bestir myself on one presupposition only.'

'You're laying down conditions of saving my life?'

'You've taunted me enough,' Smahil said savagely. 'Either you become mine, body and soul mine, or I let you die.'

'You too want my soul?'

He refused to smile. 'I've waited some years,' he said and he was only just moving his lips when he spoke.

'Holiest Heaven, Smahil, what are you asking from both of us! I'm not damning your soul and mine, if indeed they're not already damned.'

Smahil shrugged tightly. 'Your lily soul or your death at midnight, Cija.'

'I don't believe you. Or, if I do, still I can't. I refuse to believe you. Smahil! Is this you? Have I really ever known you? You've always treated me as a reasonable human being, admitted one or two individual rights to be my rights as they are anyone's . . . How can you ask of me what you know is vile sin, when you hold such power over me, and refuse me any choice to answer no?'

'I love you,' he said. He was furious.

'No love would survive such a situation as you would force me into. I would hate, I would loathe you.'

'Your loathing will do,' he said. 'It's yours.'

'Save me, if it is easy as you say for you, and talk to me afterwards. How can you drive me to such a terrible choice?'

'Even at the brink of the grave, you are negative.' Smahil now was whispering, his eyes dilating as they moved over me, unable to rest at any point. 'If this is your eternality, then be the nothing you wish. You have lost the life you refused to be born to, little one.' Smahil turned away. I saw that even the pupils of his eyes were white with fury.

Then Smahil turned, he left me. His cloak swirled, touched me, and burned where it touched.

From among the priests a fair thickset girl moved quickly to take his arm.

The priests closed about me.

*

A fraction before midnight all the trumpets snarled. A gong shook the pyramid and the worms raced amongst their roots. The priests took me up to the hill.

The open air pulsed like wine. I heard the creakings as the bridge was lowered away from the chasm. Now there would be only the never-ending floor of sea to receive me when I was pitched into the crack of my doom. The cords they'd bound me with bit into my wrists and my breasts and behind my knees. He will come, I said to myself, and then I found my lips were moving. Smahil will not leave me to this.

Well, Smahil did turn up. Suddenly he was amongst us. He was alone.

There was chanting, the stars made frost in my brother's eyes. A priest handed him a knife and without looking at me he knelt before the High Priest for the ceremony of the consecration.

I was lying bound spread-eagled against a rock very worn and pitted and rusty, which some centuries ago had been brought from the North where the blue sub-humans used it for an altar.

The stars spat in my eyes. Smahil had arrived alone.

Then there was noise. There was shouting.

The priests, flagellating themselves with their chant, hardly heard. Their eyelids were swollen, their lips bruised, they were whole in their own hypnosis. But our Father heard and his long head turned to the disturbance beside the long head of the sacred alligator.

Bound outstaring constellations no longer existing fifty million light-years ago, I heard the bright ships beach, I heard the horror of the beach-guards at this blasphemy, I heard the clash of this steel on that and the imbecile gurgles of men dying and the rustle of the wind in the climbing fern-trees.

The High Priest drew back his arm with the great knife curving at its end.

'I expected this treachery,' he smiled at Smahil. 'Your blood, too, is acceptable.'

I prayed. A fervour of exaltation all but broke the cords. I knew he would not see me die.

As the priest's hand knotted for the stab, as the chanting priests swayed, Smahil with a wrestler's twist crouched abruptly forward under the knife and then there was the High Priest gliding through the air and the alligator hiccupping into her necklaces with discreet bewilderment.

The priests' eyes bulged through their chanting. Frost appeared on their lips and like the man who walks two steps while his head rolls from the executing sword, they completed their verse before howling and falling upon Smahil.

It was only by the noise that I could tell how the new soldiers were leaping up the pyramid or being thrust back.

I raised my neck again, clenching all my jaw muscles in a gullet-strain, but the confused fighters before my altar were all flapping gowns. I could make out neither Smahil nor the High Priest. All I saw were, out in the blackness, hundreds of horizontal red flashes. These were incomprehensible, devil-flashes in the dark, till I could see they were the light-caught knives between the teeth of the climbing soldiers.

I let my head sink back.

I had just been able to make out that the soldiers could not be reinforcements ordered by Smahil before he came here. He had not double-crossed the priest. They weren't his Northerners – they were in the pink and green uniform of my Mother.

The cord was biting into my neck. My ears throbbed and seemed to have swollen inside to fill my head.

Then there was a face right above me. A maniacal mask – that horrible facelessness that comes to the face of fanatic turned madman.

One of the priests had determined that the carnage should not deflect the purpose of the summit. The sacrifice must be carried through.

I tried again to raise myself against the cords.

The priest held in his hand the knife the priest had blessed for Smahil to kill me with. But first the priest was girding up his robe. The hairs on his long blotched white thighs stood out like spider-hairs in the light of the torch-flares. This also was needful on the altar. *Had Smahil been going to – ?*

Two hands caught the priest's throat from behind. He jerked back, cursing, not just swearing, a proper priestly curse on the life and happiness of his attacker. But the hands cut short the curse in a series of bubbles. The priest's mouth drenched my feet with blood and he fell.

The attacker, not Smahil but one of my Mother's sergeants, dragged him off me. With deft swipes of his belt-knife he broke those cords. I still couldn't move my hands or legs.

The sergeant helped me to my feet.

When he saw how the ropes had disfigured my flesh he chafed and rubbed me. He was in a hurry. 'Come on, lass, hold up, bear up, move, try and move,' he kept saying, glancing about, supporting me with one arm. I hopped two steps and did not quite stumble. The sergeant began to help me down.

Then the sergeant was no longer there. He had pitched forward and from below came a plunge and splash as the deep waters were pierced.

I had not thought my Father so active.

Turning, his lips drew back in the smile a wolf gives.

'So, child,' he said, nearer acknowledging me than at any other time, 'you thought to escape with a whole skin and soul intact?'

He laid his hand on me. I bit him, hating my teeth for the contact. He didn't flinch at all.

'Down below,' he said. 'We're keeping you for later.'

A great fan of fronds rose quivering before us, a fern taller than either of us with a trunk like a tree. My Father drew me into the depths. The tendrils trembled on our faces. Then in the very midst we stepped down, and there was a tunnel of utter dark, and stone about us echoing in that dark. We wound downwards.

Now as we went I heard sharp feet and a slither as of chainmail in the dark tunnel winding behind us. I said nothing. I hoped the pursuer would kill my Father even if I were victim too. But at a turn of the tunnel my Father seized from a wall-sconce a torch the turning had hidden from our view, and as he lifted and held it I looked back and saw the alligator mistress following us with its snout out and its eyes poking over its jewels and my flesh crawled.

We did not come out into the place with the floating throne. We wound and wound, cutting through the black earth, and snakes looped quicksilver in the torch-glare from our path, and some of the stones in the walls were not stones, they were white skulls.

My Father seemed to be intent on entering even the City from below. I knew that at one great stretch we had passed beneath the river. The walls dripped green moisture and green fungus indistinguishable the one from the other. A rushing was constant at a height above us, and the ceiling wept.

We were in familiar passages, filigreed and tiled.

A green light shone and the wall opened. At the same time a crepitation of far cacophony rustled to us, the little tinny squeaking sounds of far-off rampage and bloodshed.

In the wall-opening shone a figure too tall to be a woman, and yet a woman. The mist surrounding her shimmered and my Father tightened his grip on my tortured wrist and he stood. I saw a smile flickering like a flame around his lips.

'You are using my places for your own,' the woman whispered. 'Go another way to your Temple and your riot.'

'You have too long lain coiled at the heart of the deep places, Old One,' my Father said. 'Go back.'

'Leave my places, false priest,' the words softly grazed the witch's mouth.

My Father stood so tall the tunnel cowered. His robes seemed to shine out a cruel white light. He raised his arm and power pointed along it as he raised it to the witch. I knew no way to save her. I had by now despairing respect for my Father's power.

Yet before the power blasted and shrivelled her, the witch whispered one word. I heard the word, yet it slid off my memory. I remember only the writhing with which it fled her mouth. But the alligator in the following shadows knew the ancient command. And as the white light flashed from my Father's arm, and the witch fell silently, the length of the reptile was resistless upon my Father, he was flung to the tiles, the jewelled snout and the endless teeth of his paramour were busy in him, and his long shrieks rang again and again down the empty corridors.

With a rather nasty feeling like my blood curdling somewhere in the region of my throat, I turned to fly, to race away, and yet I stayed. The tail-thrashing reptile was for a space unaware of anything but the plaything that had been its master. The witch lay twisted. The raising of my Father's arm had charred the floss from her body. Her face was burnt. I could make out no features but the mouth, whole, a split like a plum's in the lower lip. The breasts jutted like young hills. The flesh of the nipples was uncurled and pink as fresh cherries, yet she had been one of the Changeless, centuries here in the dark, and I have seen the nipples of young women after use curl like lamb-fur. There was that faint girdle, that groove about the lower part of the flesh of her belly, that is called the girdle of the love-daemon and that only passionate women have. The bones of her pelvis stood out above the small hollows where blue veins branched in the cream of her groin. Her thighs did not meet, which is the mark they look for in the slave-markets of the Southern bazaars. Yet this perfection, this wholesome passionate envelope had stayed austere, unmarked, watchful, alone long aeons here in the lonely dark under the earth.

There was nothing I could do. The flesh was empty.

The alligator gurgled in the mass of my Father.

I ran to the Temple, I ran to the rioting, the pillaging and slaughter of the mob.

*

The Temple was being stormed.

It was defended not only by priests but by the faithful populace. But those who favoured the Dictatress against the High Priest were looting and setting fire where they could. There was fire in the ancient arras. There was blood on the holy high altar that had known only the blood of sacrificial murder.

I pushed my way, unnoticed, to the door but couldn't get out into the carnage of the courtyard. I looked back into the building. The tapestry all along one crystal wall was aflicker with little tongues of flame that made the patterns come alive while they smouldered. In the gallery above the fighters, the Temple children watched gleefully.

In a surge of fighters I made it out into the courtyard.

Here the going was quite easy for anyone who wasn't intent on violence. Scores of women, in fact, motherly-looking souls on a night out, were scurrying and weaving past the horrors, each clasping some sacred chalice or crystal stool or onyx candlestick which would feed her family a month by the courtesy of the Gods.

It was here I saw Rubila, the brothel Mam, sailing proud-prowed with armfuls of this and that. Leading the loot-laden donkey, her son Eel was with her. And so was that little waif who has so often haunted my conscience – I've forgotten her name, the little respectable business-girl who told me in her sad reedy little accent how terrible it is to be prisoner to the commerce of other people's lust. In spite of the danger of being nabbed by Eel or his ghastly Mam, I was about to dash over and urge Aka to get out *now* when suddenly I realised that Aka, yes that's her little name, was quite free to do this for herself, was in fact hardly observed by her employer-jailers and that all three were darting in and out (Mam rather ponderously) and seizing anything of value on the bodies of the dead or helpless.

184

Now someone did bear down on me and to my amazement it was Mother.

'Cija!' she cried. She was very round-eyed.

'Well, well, well! I never thought to see you again. Lovely manners, may I say, pissing off like that in the middle of someone's dinner-party leaving other people to wash and feed your brat. Have you seen either of the girls? I don't like Urga to be out on her own now. Oh, the disgrace of it if she suffered a miscarriage on the public highway!'

'She's pregnant by the Major?' I deduced. My heart slipped. 'Where is Seka? I never meant to leave her, it was all most unavoidable – '

Mother's agitation had drawn eyes to us and now Eel's Mam let out a siren scream and wallowed gracefully over to us.

I thought she'd got her beady eyes on me again. But she and Mother sank into each other's arms and embraced.

'Titia!' Mam cried, and Mother shrieked 'Rubila!'

'I haven't seen Titia since she left our establishment before you was born!' Rubila cried to the uninterested Eel. I was forgotten. I skirted them and made off to the gates. The house will be empty, I thought. I'll go and get Seka.

It was empty, so empty I doubted she'd be there. The shutters swung. The door creaked on a broken hinge, and Father's job-lot antlers had been dropped on the path between the trampled flower-borders. Looters had been here while the family were out on a looting spree.

The compost heap had been thoroughly turned over to make sure it hid no valuables. I don't think the robbers had found anything. But I stooped as I saw something. A boot, not just exactly like one of Gurul's – it *was* one of Gurul's, even the slash was there where the netting had scraped his foot in his backing away from the witch's beasts. And here was a finger-bone, and on the finger-bone a ring I recognised. And, yes, there the remains of a something that obviously, once you *knew*, had been a little monkey.

So that was what Father had done with his unwelcome

185

visitors who had never called again. I was only sorry the monkey had to go too. I suppose if it had made its way back alone, more suspicion would have been roused than at Gurul's own absence.

So that was what made our feast the night Smahil came to supper.

I must get Seka. Let Seka be there in the house.

But now hands fell on me.

'It's she,' men in uniform grunted.

# PART SIX

# MY MOTHER'S SAFE PALACE

Now I have back both my daughter and my Diary, and it's very nice of course to sit in the secure sunlight on a secure circular private lawn aglint with sunbeams and garden insects like chips of shattered glass and write while the child chases her turtle in the dimpled pool.

They brought me with all honour to my Mother and my Mother was so pleased.

'Cija, Cija, girl of my heart!' She clasped me to her and when I was released there were brooch-patterns and necklace-patterns all over me, I had been pressed so ardently.

'What happened?' I asked her after all the delight could decently be abated.

'Garments for my daughter, silks for my daughter, wines, meats, music!' The slaves obeyed pretty smartly but just out of general enthusiasm my Mother's whip flicked out and curled round a leg or two for encourage-ment.

'We are in complete control of our City, my daughter. Can you imagine? His body has just been found, chewed up, in a subterranean deep. A bit mangled, with an oddly embellished alligator crouching possessively over it, but the face was recognisable and I've had it shown above the City walls and that's quelled the last of the *faithful*.' My Mother's pug face twisted in a fearsome sneer as she dis-missed the religious among her populace.

'Well, Cija, and so you're safe and sound, my angel? At last I have you at my side again. Oh, we shall see some rare times.'

'How did the men know to bring me to you?'

'I had them out looking for you, dear.'

'Please *explain*, Mother,' I shouted.

'About sunset a little fat girl came to me and demanded private audience. She used such potent passwords that after first ordering her turned away I recalled the order – I was busy but had perhaps best see what meddling she was party to. She was a lady-in-waiting and she said she knew by means she couldn't disclose that at midnight my daughter would be sacrificed on the old devil's toy pyramid. I had no inkling you were within the land! I gave my orders straight away and it has all worked out quite nicely.'

'But *why* did Katisa get you to save me?'

'Yes, I asked her that too. She knew, she said, by all these secret private means she couldn't disclose, that you had promised to "belong" as she genteelly or perhaps melo-dramatically put it, to a Northern Major called Smahil on condition he saved you at this busy midnight.'

'But I promised Smahil no such thing!'

'Well, the little lady was in quite a dither about this promise she swore she knew all about but couldn't divulge the means of. She said that her reason for ratting to me was that if you were saved by *my* men you needn't keep the promise, which she thought you weren't too anxious to do anyway.'

'She needn't have bothered. Smahil had no intention of saving me. Even the High Priest expected treachery from him, but Smahil came alone to carry out my last cere-mony.'

'Who is this Smahil, Cija? I know he's the Northern Major, but I seem to remember I sent a pale-haired foster-son of one of my ladies off with you as hostage when the dear dragon-General first carried you off in his hot-headed way.'

'The same Smahil. My brother, Mother, by that mangled High Priest and the waiting-woman Ooldra.'

'Wonders never cease,' my Mother very equably said, for in fact wherever she is they seem to cease automati-cally.

'And Katisa must be weeping her eyes out now that her

188

double-cross was all for nothing and has spread in such gonging repercussions,' I said.

'I had her tossed in the bear-pit,' my Mother said comfortably. 'I don't like that sort of back-biting.'

A table was set before us and slaves poured wines like garnets and jade liquidised.

'I have a daughter,' I said through a mouthful of roast pterosaur wrapped in jellied sour-cream. 'She can't speak, but I want her.'

'You've made me a grandmother. I suppose it had to come. I'll have her fetched if you should happen to know where she is,' my Mother offered.

'Yes. She is – '

'Is she Zerd's child?'

'Zerd's? Yes.'

'That's good. Zerd will be pleased.'

'Oh, he knew about her when she was to be born.'

'I mean he'll be glad to see her now.'

The banqueting hall turned dim. The candles became livid. I stared at my Mother's face which seemed to have retreated a dimension.

'Zerd? Here?'

'Within the month, child. He sent word he's on his way from Atlan to overthrow his insolent father-in-law and of course he'll be based here, among friends. What a very very pleasant surprise for him to find you here,' my Mother said with a cat-complacence and no sign at all of the airy carelessness that was only in her voice.

'Mother! I can't face him – '

'Pho. You're married, aren't you? Where are you to run off to this time, what ridiculous silly place will you choose to die in most probably? Of course you must face him. Dignity must be the order of the day. He's bringing Sedili, that Northern camp-tramp.'

'She's his legal wife.'

'Legal? When you were crowned his consort? Talk sense, child.'

'I've officially left him, Mother.'

'Oh, you annoy me, you infuriate me, Cija, will you

189

never learn? Was he such a bad husband? I've heard that to Sedili and Lara both he was a model husband. Was he ever unfaithful without buying you a little gift?'

'He divorced me.' I lied desperately.

'As far as he's concerned, marriage is grounds for divorce,' my Mother grumbled. 'What did he want to divorce a daughter of mine for? You'll be proud and disdainful, but not exactly unwelcoming, when he arrives, you understand that.'

*

It's the sweetest of luxuries to sing in the bath without that crippling fear of being overheard. I sit and swash and hum till my teeth vibrate, thinking how tender and beauteous one's voice can be in any hollow reverberant place with tiles. But I am worried about one thing. In the Tower, that was my cradle and nearly my grave, I was glad of this irregular timing, because blood to the apes was a curiosity with an excitement of its own. But now I am long overdue. I loved Ung-g the first-man. I shall not call court physicians to butcher his blossoming from my body. But when Zerd comes, I hope my Mother shields me from his wrath when he finds that I am giving Seka a little brother whose father was less human than Zerd is.

All Futura Books are available at your bookshop or newsagent, or can be ordered from the following address:
Futura Books, Cash Sales Department.
P.O. Box 11, Falmouth, Cornwall.

Please send cheque or postal order (no currency), and allow 55p for postage and packing for the first book plus 22p for the second book and 14p for each additional book ordered up to a maximum charge of £1.75 in U.K

Customers in Eire and B.F.P.O. please allow 55p for the first book, 22p for the second book plus 14p per copy for the next 7 books, thereafter 8p per book.

Overseas customers please allow £1 for postage and packing for the first book and 25p per copy for each additional book.